Lark gazed at Dash as their bodies moved to the beat.

The more she watched him, the more she realized how much she was falling for the young designer. Even though he was at least ten years younger than she, he was mature beyond his age. If Lark was ever going to find love, then she would have to take a leap of faith and trust that Dash felt the same way.

Here goes, she thought as she danced closer and draped her arms around his neck.

Lark searched his eyes, trying to get a read on him as she moved her body against his.

Dash didn't shy away. He took her by the waist and hugged her tightly.

Lark exhaled. She felt safe and secure within his arms and let her inhibitions go. Although the beat of the music was fast, they began slow dancing to a rhythm of their own.

Lark closed her eyes and rested her head on Dash's shoulder. She was so close to him that she could smell the scent of his cologne. Lark nuzzled her nose closer and took a deep breath…

Dear Reader,

Thank you so much for picking up a copy of
Season for Love!

Sometimes we overlook that one person who is offering
us love, for one reason or the other. It could be a
difference in age, or maybe a forbidden work liaison,
much like Lark and Dash. In Lark's case, when she gives
herself permission to be happy, she falls head over heels in
love with the stunning younger man.

Season for Love is a story full of romance and a bit of
intrigue. There is someone from Lark's past who crops up
at the most inopportune time. But with Dash by her side,
Lark's nemesis has his work cut out for him!

Stay tuned for my next titillating novel!

Happy reading,

Velvet Carter

SEASON *For* LOVE

VELVET CARTER

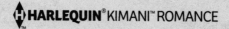

HARLEQUIN® KIMANI™ ROMANCE

Recycling programs
for this product may
not exist in your area.

ISBN-13: 978-0-373-86386-0

Season for Love

HARLEQUIN®
™ www.Harlequin.com

Printed in U.S.A.

Velvet Carter is not just the name of a luxurious fabric, but it's also the name of one of the world's leading writers of "exotica." She's a prolific novelist, who paints pictures with her words. Velvet has her finger on the pulse and knows how to make your heart race with her tantalizing stories filled with romance and seduction. Her novels have been translated into German, and released in London to critical acclaim. Velvet uses the world as her muse, traveling the globe for provocative inspiration.

Books by Velvet Carter

Harlequin Kimani Romance

Blissfully Yours
Season for Love

Visit the Author Profile page at
Harlequin.com for more titles

To Earl Milloy and Terry Brantley,
two "Good Brothers" whom I not only
had the pleasure of knowing, but of loving!
You guys will truly be missed, beyond words!

Acknowledgments

I'd like to thank the team at Harlequin, especially
Shannon Criss and Caroline Acebo for your insightful
edits that really helped flesh out the story! And to my
wonderful agent, Sara Camilli, you are the best!

To my family and friends who understand when I have
to go undercover, lock myself in a room and create
another page-turner!

And to my mom, Alline Carter, whom I love dearly!

Peace and Blessings!

Velvet

Chapter 1

Lark Randolph was taking a long, relaxing bubble bath, complete with soft music, candles and a glass of crisp chardonnay. After a long, stressful day at the office, she was now pampering herself before her much-anticipated date. It had been a while since Lark enjoyed a night out with a man, and the possibilities of that evening made a smile form on her lips. As she lounged in the warm, fragrant water, she fantasized about this guy being The One. Although she hadn't had much success with relationships, Lark hadn't given up hope of finding her soul mate.

She lathered soapy suds all over her skin with an oblong loofah. After gently rubbing her body, she rinsed off and stepped out of the Jacuzzi tub. Lark toweled off, wrapped herself in a white terry-cloth robe and made her way into the adjacent bedroom. Spread out on the king-size bed were a black cocktail dress with a plunging neckline and a multistranded pearl necklace. She was going for a sexy yet sophisticated look for the evening, much like Audrey Hepburn in *Breakfast at Tiffany's*.

Being a workaholic, Lark hadn't put too much emphasis on finding a man and cultivating a relationship. This had culminated in a string of short-lived involvements. As the years ticked by, while most of her friends got married and started families, she focused on growing her family's fashion-design business. Despite some challenges, Randolph on the Runway was still one of the industry's leading designers of women's clothing.

Lark was in her late thirties. She knew if she didn't shift her attention from her work to her personal life and put in a concerted effort to find a husband, then the family she had always dreamed about would probably elude her forever. Lark was determined that would not be her destiny. In the past, friends had set her up on blind dates but nothing had materialized.

To hasten her search to find a mate, Lark had followed the trend and had joined several online dating sites. She was serious—she had mapped out a plan and was approaching the electronic dating process like a business. She would spend her evenings scanning profiles of men whom she found visually appealing. Lark took her time and closely read their answers to various stock questions designed for compatibility. She took notes and didn't waste time deleting those men who had nothing to offer but a pretty face. Once she narrowed down her search, she devised the next step.

Before meeting a potential candidate, she would communicate with him via email. If the electronic exchanges went well, Lark would agree to talk on the phone with him. And if the conversation flowed, she would have a face-to-face meeting with him, usually at a coffee shop over a cappuccino or a latte. If there was chemistry between them, Lark would agree to dinner with her prospect.

Lark was excited about tonight's date. Edwin Spears, a mature, successful investment banker, was the third man she had met online, but the only one she had actually met in person. The first two guys hadn't even passed the preliminary email test. Their lewd comments had alluded to getting her between the sheets. Lark had wasted no time in setting them straight. She had zero interest in a one-night stand.

After a nice online chat with Edwin, they had agreed to meet over coffee one afternoon, and it had lasted for hours. She and Edwin had covered the basic getting-to-know-you questions—Where are you from? What school did you attend? What do you do for a living? Do you golf or play tennis?—and had talked explicitly about their individual future plans. They both wanted to eventually get married and raise a family. Edwin was candid and refreshing. During their first conversation, Lark had asked him point-blank if he was involved with anyone else, to which he had emphatically replied, "No!"

Lark had been relieved. She had a rule never to date someone else's man. She believed a man could only be unfaithful if he had a willing partner to cheat with. Lark didn't care how many sob stories she heard about a man's marriage being on the rocks, putting him on the verge of filing for divorce. Or the line to beat all lines: *My wife and I have an understanding.* As far as Lark was concerned, marriage was marriage, whether happy or not.

Over the next few weeks, Lark had found Edwin to be consistent and considerate. He had phoned every evening to ask about her day. She looked forward to hearing his sexy baritone voice and often fantasized about him lying in bed cuddled next to her. He'd sent bouquets of white roses to her office, with notes that read "I'm thinking about you." After a month of Edwin's steady calls and old-fashioned courting, Lark began warming up to him, even though she had seen him only once. Lark didn't think this was odd since they both had demanding careers. Edwin had told her that he didn't want to plan their first date until he completed a major deal he had been working on. Lark totally understood. She even told her best friend, Darcy, that he might be The One.

Darcy had warned Lark to tread cautiously. Darcy said that she had read numerous articles about the hazards of internet dating and that some people used those sites like an electronic meat market, looking for sex partners. Lark had halfheartedly listened to her friend's advice. She knew Darcy had stern opinions when it came to the business of dating.

Lark finished dressing, slipped on a pair of black Jimmy Choo shoes to complete her look, combed her chin-length auburn hair and applied her makeup. She dabbed the backs of her earlobes with the sexy scent of Burberry's Brit Eau de Parfum before leaving.

Outside, she hailed a taxi in front of her condo building and headed over to Jean-Georges, the swanky Michelin award–winning restaurant located in the Trump International Hotel & Tower. Edwin had chosen the restaurant and made the reservations. He had told Lark not to worry about any of the details, just to meet him at the restaurant looking beautiful. Lark loved a man who could take control and make plans on his own. In her past relationships she had been the one to orchestrate the details of dates, so needing simply to show up was a welcome change.

Lark could feel her heart beating quickly with excitement as she exited the taxi and made her way up the steps to the entrance of the restaurant.

"Welcome to Jean-Georges. Do you have a reservation?" the tall, model-looking hostess asked.

"Yes, table for two for Spears," Lark answered, using Edwin's last name, which rolled off her tongue with ease. *"Mrs. Lark Spears"—I like the sound of that,* she thought, getting ahead of herself.

The hostess scanned the reservation book and then said, "Right this way."

Once again, excitement flowed through Lark's veins with each step she took. She was looking forward to sharing a gourmet meal with Edwin and lingering over after-dinner drinks—and maybe, just maybe, going back to her place. She wasn't ready to sleep with Edwin yet, but she wasn't opposed to other forms of intimacy. During their coffee date, she had taken notice of Edwin's full lips and had wondered whether or not he was a good kisser. Lark was sure tonight she would find out the answer.

"Here's your table. Your waiter will be right over," the hostess said, placing menus on the table.

"Thank you."

Lark sat down. She was a bit disappointed that Edwin hadn't arrived ahead of her. He always called her at the designated time. She automatically assumed that he would be prompt for their long-awaited romantic evening.

"Hello, my name is Jeff, and I'll be your waiter this

evening. Can I start you off with a cocktail or a glass of wine?"

"I'll have a Manhattan."

"Coming right up."

Lark peered around the restaurant. It was mostly filled with couples having cozy dinners. She was the only person sitting alone, and she began to feel self-conscious. *I wonder what's keeping Edwin. Maybe he got caught up in traffic.* Lark glanced at her watch. It was a quarter past eight.

She took out her cell phone and dialed his number. It rang and rang before going to voice mail. Instead of leaving a message, Lark sent him a text, thinking he would get her message sooner.

Hey where r u? I'm @ Jean-Georges waiting 4 u.

The waiter came back with her cocktail. "Would you like to hear about tonight's specials?"

Lark looked at the front entrance, hoping to see Edwin walking through the door, but he was nowhere in sight. "Actually, I'm waiting for someone. Can you come back in a few minutes?"

"Sure, no problem."

Ten minutes passed with no sign of Edwin. Lark was starting to worry. *Maybe he was in a car accident.* She called his phone again. This time it went straight to voice mail without ringing, an indication that his phone was turned off.

"Hi, Edwin. It's me, Lark. Where are you? I hope you're okay. I'm at the restaurant waiting. See you soon."

Another ten minutes passed. The waiter returned and Lark ordered another drink to ease her nerves. She had read the menu twice, trying to bide her time. Worry began to turn to disappointment and disappointment to anger at the thought of Edwin standing her up. Lark ran a company dependent on deadlines and she considered time to be a precious commodity. The thought of someone wasting hers was unacceptable.

Lark took the phone out of her purse and dialed Edwin's number again. She was now fuming. She was going to give him a piece of her mind for not showing up for their date.

"Hello?" a female voice answered on the first ring.

"Oh…I must have the wrong number," Lark said.

"No, Lark, you have the right number. Edwin won't be joining you at Jean-Georges tonight or any other night."

Lark's mouth fell open. She was speechless. "Who is this?" she finally said.

"I'm Edwin's fiancée. I read your text and listened to your message. I don't know what Edwin has been telling you, but he's taken. Please don't ever call this number again."

The line went dead before Lark had a chance to respond. She sat there, staring at her phone in total disbelief.

"Are you still waiting, miss?" the waiter asked, standing at the side of her table.

"Uh…no… No, I'm not."

As the waiter rattled off the names of the gourmet entrées, Lark stared into space. She couldn't believe the sudden turn of events. The words *I'm Edwin's fiancée* kept reverberating in her ear. Lark was dumbfounded. She had totally misjudged Edwin's character. He had lied to her about being single. Not only was he not single, but he was engaged to be married! His intention was probably to have no-strings-attached sex with her—as Darcy had warned—but he was taking the slow, drawn-out approach.

"Excuse me, miss… Would you care to order now?" the waiter asked after he had finished explaining the specials of the evening.

"I'm sorry," Lark said, coming back to reality. "Can you repeat the specials?"

After the waiter reiterated his spiel, Lark ordered.

"I'll have the salmon, medium rare. And can you bring me a glass of champagne?"

"Right away, miss."

After the waiter brought the champagne over, Lark slightly raised the glass and whispered, "Here's to the end of my online dating career."

She wasn't about to sit there crying her eyes out and mourning the loss of a potential relationship. As far as she was concerned, it was Edwin's loss, not hers. Lark knew she had a lot to offer the right man, and obviously Edwin was not that man.

Chapter 2

The Seventh Avenue offices of Randolph on the Runway—RR—were bustling with activity. The fall shows were over and the company was busy filling the last of the orders, designing a new line and preparing for the next round of fashion shows.

Being the chief operating officer and creative director, Lark was right in the thick of things. She strutted briskly down the corridor in a snug black pencil skirt, a white cotton shirt with huge billowy sleeves and a pair of pointy black stilettos. Her short hair was tucked behind her ears and her lips were painted blood-orange, her signature color, which was a blend of two different lipsticks. Lark spoke quickly to her assistant, Angelica, as she walked alongside her.

Although the fall fashion shows were long over, Lark had recently called some of the buyers she knew personally and had been able to convince them to purchase a few pieces. The sales numbers had been dwindling over the past few seasons and she desperately needed to increase revenue before the company drowned in debt.

"Do we have the final sales numbers yet from Patricia Taylor?" Patricia was one of the buyers whom Lark had contacted.

"No, but I'm sure I'll have them later this afternoon," Angelica responded.

"Okay, sounds good. What time is my next interview scheduled for?"

Angelica referred to her tablet and said, "Two o'clock."

Lark had been meeting with some of the hottest designers on Seventh Avenue. She had let go of her lead designer and was having a difficult time finding his replacement. Most of the candidates she had met with either didn't have the design skills or the right vision for her company. And with profits plummeting, she needed a designer who not only had major cutting-edge talent, but whom she could work with in harmony.

As she made her way to the conference room, she reflected back on the incident that had sparked the blowup with the previous designer.

Lark and Sebastian, the lead designer, who had been with Randolph on the Runway for years, had been in the company's showroom scrutinizing the collection just days before the start of the fall show. He had wanted to pull the final piece from the collection, saying the hemline was dated and the gown didn't fit in with his designs. Lark completely disagreed. She respected Sebastian's opinion, but she felt strongly about her design. What started off as a civil disagreement quickly turned into a screaming match, with them going toe-to-toe, neither one giving an inch.

"This piece is passé!" Sebastian sniped, plucking at the rose-colored taffeta gown. "And who uses this fabric any longer?"

"No, it's not passé. I designed this piece myself and I think it's perfect for the grand finale.

"This gown gives the line a touch of elegance. I realize that taffeta is a material from a time long ago, but I want to re-create a 1940s-type feeling. A time of romance, and this gown depicts that era perfectly," Lark said.

"Romance is overrated, and this gown's above-the-ankle hemline is off-putting to say the least. Maybe you should stick to being the COO, hire a creative director and leave the designing to us professionals."

"I have a degree from FIT in fashion design as well as an MBA from Harvard. I'm more than capable of running this company *and* designing a gown!" Lark sniped.

"Obviously your creative side isn't as developed as your business side." He took the dress off the rack and held it in his hands. "Look at this thing. The color is dull. The neckline is too high. Basically, it's…it's…just horrendous!"

Lark was quiet for a moment. "Why are you being so nasty, Sebastian? We've always worked so well together. What's wrong? Are you having some type of personal issues? Did you and Peter break up?"

"He moved out, but I'm perfectly fine. My love life has never affected my work. Why are you trying to overrule me? I'm the lead designer. Or have you forgotten?"

His nasty remark incensed Lark. There was only so much more she could take from him. "And I run this company. Or have you forgotten?"

"Without my fabulous creations, RR would just be another wannabe design company manufacturing run-of-the-mill dresses," he said.

Lark could feel her blood pressure rising. Not only was he insulting her design ability, but he was now also insulting the company her grandfather had founded. "That's enough, Sebastian. This conversation is over!"

He clenched the gown in his hands. "No. What's over is this hideous thing you call a gown. I'm not putting it in the show."

"That's not your call, Sebastian. As the creative director, the final word is mine," Lark said, getting more frustrated by the second.

"Like I said before, you need to stick to management and leave the designing to the professionals," he reiterated, further insulting his boss.

She took a deep breath in an effort to calm down. Their disagreement had gotten out of hand and it was time to put it to an end. She counted to ten in her head. Lark lowered her voice and measured her words. "Sebastian, the gown is going into the show…period. End of discussion."

"If you put that *thing* in the show, it'll ruin the collection. A collection I worked so hard to perfect, and I refuse to let that happen." Sebastian began ripping the seams of the gown with his bare hands, destroying what Lark had created.

"Stop! What are you doing? You're ruining my dress! You're…you're fired!" Lark screamed.

"You can't fire me. I have a contract!" he said arrogantly.

"I can, and I did." Lark exhaled. "Obviously your business side isn't as developed as your creative side. There's a clause in your contract that allows the company to buy you out at any given time—a clause that I designed, by the way. So you can pack up your things and leave today!"

Sebastian stood there in shock. He opened his mouth to speak, but he didn't utter a sound. Finally he said, "What about the show?"

"Not your problem anymore. I think you need to start your own company, since you have such strong opinions on designs. It's unfortunate, but we can no longer work together. I'll have security escort you to your office so you can get your personal things." Lark started to leave, but she turned back.

"In case you didn't understand the legal jargon in the contract, there's also a clause that states all of the designs you created while employed by RR are company property. If you try to take any sketchbooks or upload company files, I'll have no choice but to sue you for breach of contract."

"We'll see about that! You can't get rid of me that easily! I've invested too much time and energy in this company to just walk away."

"You don't have a choice," Lark said calmly.

Sebastian made a hissing sound and stormed out of the room.

Lark hadn't intended to fire Sebastian that day, but she wasn't going to allow anyone to speak down to her and treat her with such blatant disrespect. Lark was more than a fair boss, and she didn't have problems with any of the other employees. Although she ran a tight ship, the work environment at Randolph on the Runway was creative and productive.

"What's the name of the designer who's coming in at two?" Lark asked Angelica.

"Dash Migilio. I emailed you a copy of his résumé and bio. Also, here's a hard copy." She handed Lark a folder.

Lark opened the folder and scanned the information as she walked. "Impressive."

When they reached the conference room, a tall man dressed in a gray European-cut suit was standing at the window with his back to the door. Lark cleared her throat and he turned around.

Lark took a good look at the handsome stranger. He had curly, coal-black hair, an olive complexion and warm, greenish-brown eyes. His face looked like that of a young Warren Beatty. Lark scanned the length of his toned physique. She could feel her throat becoming parched as she stood there staring at the gorgeous man. Normally, she wasn't attracted to younger men, but this guy had her full attention.

"I'm sorry I'm early." He walked toward Lark and extended his hand. "I'm Dash Migilio."

"Hello. I'm Lark Randolph," she said, still studying his chiseled face.

"I know. I've seen your picture in the trades numerous times. It's a pleasure to finally meet you in person." He beamed a bright white smile.

Even his teeth are perfect, Lark thought. "Please have a seat. This is Angelica, my assistant, and she's going to sit in on the meeting."

"Nice to meet you, Angelica," he said, extending his hand.

And he's polite, too!

After they were seated at the conference table, Lark took a breath and refocused. She had been momentarily taken aback by his good looks and charm, but now she needed to move on to business. She glanced down at his résumé.

"I see that you interned at Ralph Lauren."

"That was during my senior year at Pratt. I worked closely with several designers there. The experience was invaluable."

"After graduation you worked with Andrew Marc for a few years."

"Yes, I was a junior designer and learned a great deal about the outerwear business."

"You've only been employed by male designers. Do you have a problem working with women?" she asked point-blank.

"Not at all," he said, smiling.

Ohh...I could get lost in that smile of his.

Lark cleared her throat, trying to free her mind of unprofessional thoughts. "There's a twelve-month gap on your résumé. Why?" she asked.

"I spent a year in Italy at my family's estate. I'm a first-generation New Yorker. My parents are from Florence, where they own a textile mill. The plant manager had retired, so I took over until they could find his replacement. They eventually promoted the assistant manager, but I stayed on for a while. I love Italy and enjoy spending time there whenever I can."

"So you're familiar with textiles?"

"Yes. I spent many summers in the mill. I know everything there is to know about fabrics."

Lark nodded her head. She liked what she was hearing so far. "Why didn't you stay on at your family's company? Sounds like that business is in your blood."

"It is, but I'm a designer at heart. After my extended holiday, I came back to New York to continue my design career. Much like Mr. Lauren and Mr. Marc, I plan to make my own mark in this industry."

Lark immediately flashed back to her argument with Sebastian. Although she wanted a talented designer on her team, she wasn't about to hire another person who undervalued her talent. "Mr. Migilio, let me be clear from the start. As the creative director, I work closely with the lead designer. Although I'm the chief operating officer of Randolph on the Runway, I have a degree from FIT, and I design, as well."

"That's awesome," he said, flashing his one-hundred-watt smile again. "As far as I'm concerned, the bottom line should be what designs will catapult RR ahead of the rest and make our company the best in the business."

Our company? He's thinking like a team player. I like that. Lark nodded her head again. "I totally agree. Can I see your portfolio?"

"Sure." Dash reached into his leather messenger bag, retrieved a silver tablet, powered it up and handed the device to Lark.

Lark began swiping through pictures of his designs. His work was indeed impressive and unique. He had a keen eye for detail. There were pictures of women's clothing, menswear and even accessories. The more she saw, the more she wanted to see. Dash was talented beyond belief. His work was a cross between Gianni Versace and Valentino—classy with an edge.

Lark swiped her finger across the screen once more, and this time, instead of seeing another one of his unique creations, staring back at her was a picture of Dash in aqua-blue swim trunks, lying on a beach next to a pretty blonde woman in a skimpy red bikini. Lark didn't say a word. She stared at the picture, her eyes roaming over Dash's manly chest and well-defined abs. Lark could feel herself heating up as she admired his half-nude body.

"So…do you like what you see?" Dash asked.

"I sure do." Lark smiled. She swiped past his personal picture, turned off the tablet and handed it back to him. "I'd like to offer you the position of lead designer."

"That's great! I'm eager to start as soon as possible."

"I like your enthusiasm. However, the offer is contingent upon a thorough background check. If your references come back positive, then the position is yours."

"No worries there. I left on good terms with all of my former employers."

"That's good to hear. Angelica will take you to the human-resources department so you can fill out the necessary paperwork."

Dash stood up. "I look forward to working with you, Ms. Randolph."

"And I with you. Please call me Lark."

After Angelica and Dash left the conference room, Lark went over to the window and stared out. "I hope offering him the position isn't a mistake," she said underneath her breath.

Lark had reservations about working with someone she was physically attracted to. She thought about calling down to HR and rescinding her offer of employment. Lark pondered the situation for a moment instead of making a rash decision. There was no denying that Dash's talent would benefit the company, and with the new spring/summer line going into development, RR desperately needed a top designer. Besides, he was at least ten years her junior and Lark had never dated a younger man. She preferred her men to be more seasoned. And thinking back on the photo she'd seen on his tablet, he was probably in a relationship with the blonde in the picture.

Lark took a deep breath. Hiring Dash was right for the company, and with her personal life on hold for the moment, work had taken precedence once again.

Chapter 3

Dash was meeting Vance Shelton, his best friend and attorney, for a drink at the Monkey Bar, one of Manhattan's renowned bar-restaurants. Dash had completed the preliminary paperwork at Randolph on the Runway earlier that day, but he wanted his attorney to read over the contract before he signed it.

Dash arrived first and settled in at the bar, which was full of businessmen and -women, as well as wealthy older gentlemen vying for the attention of younger beauties. Dash drank his Manhattan and eavesdropped on the conversation unfolding next to him.

A silver-haired gentleman dressed sharply in black gabardine slacks and a baby-blue tailored shirt was trying to entice a buxom redhead, wearing a skimpy hot-pink dress and matching spike heels, who was perched on the stool near him.

"So...have you ever cruised on a yacht in the Mediterranean?" the silver fox asked.

"No, but I've slept on several water beds here in Manhattan," she replied, sipping her wine.

What the hell does a water bed have to do with a yacht? Dash thought as he listened.

"Well, I've got one of those on my yacht," the man said, resting his hand on her bare thigh.

Dash watched as the man ran his hand up the woman's leg and under the hem of her dress. She did not protest.

"Your glass is almost empty." The older man motioned for the bartender and then asked him, "What is she drinking?"

"Chardonnay," the bartender responded.

"Enough wine. Bring us a bottle of Dom."

"Oh, champagne! I love champagne! The bubbles tickle my nose," the woman said, giggling.

He's going to ply her with liquor, pop a little blue pill and then show her his water bed, Dash thought, shaking his head. Women with low IQs were not his cup of tea. He liked his women to be attractive *and* smart, like Lark Randolph. Dash had read about Lark's career in the industry trades over the years and had not only admired her beauty but also her accomplishments. Lark had taken her family's company from a middle-of-the-road dress manufacturer to a leading designer of womenswear.

He sipped his cocktail and thought back to their meeting. He had found it hard to concentrate on the interview while staring into her beautiful face. Her features were picture-perfect—small hazel eyes, keen nose and pouty lips. She could easily have been a model instead of COO of a thriving fashion company. Her lips were painted a lovely shade of red that enticed him with every word she spoke. Dash's mind had kept focusing on what he could do with those lips outside of the boardroom and in the bedroom.

In preparation for his interview, Dash had searched Lark's name online. He had learned that after graduating from college, Lark had worked as a junior designer at Randolph on the Runway, under the tutelage of Darcy McCay, the lead designer at the time. Lark had learned every aspect of the business from the older designer. She had even gone back to school and earned an MBA from Harvard, which Dash found to be quite impressive.

Dash had had his pick of design firms with which to interview after he returned from Italy, but Randolph on the Runway had been his first choice. Lark Randolph had a stellar reputation in the industry for being an astute businesswoman and designer in her own right. He had wanted to meet her in person. Lark had said that his offer of employment was contingent upon his background check. Dash didn't have any skeletons in his closet to worry about. It was only a matter of time before he was designing closely with the strikingly beautiful woman.

Working in his family's textile mill during the summers of his youth, Dash had learned early on not to mix business with pleasure. He had gotten burned once, when he briefly dated one of the other employees. She had wanted a relationship, and at the time he had wanted nothing more than a quick fling.

From then on, Dash vowed to keep his personal life and business life completely separate. But being in close proximity to a knockout like Lark, keeping his vow was going to be a challenge.

As Dash waited for Vance to arrive, he took out his tablet and browsed through the portfolio he had shown Lark, in order to get a jump on design ideas for RR's spring/summer line.

"Oh, shit!" he said underneath his breath when he saw the picture of himself and Heather lying on the beach in Italy. *I'll bet Lark saw this picture.*

Heather and Dash had met in design school and had dated the last two years of college. They both had similar interests—both were talented designers and loved to travel—and they had quickly fallen in love. He'd had every intention of proposing while they were visiting his family in Italy—he'd even bought a three-carat diamond ring—but he hadn't followed through. Unbeknownst to Heather, Dash had overheard one of her phone conversations while she was standing on the balcony in the guest room of his parents' home overlooking a grove of lemon trees.

"No, I haven't asked him yet… Yes…I promise I'm going to tell Dash the truth tonight. I love you, too, babe. 'Bye."

"Tell me the truth about what?" Dash had said, walking out onto the balcony where Heather was standing.

She whipped around. "Uh…Dash…hi."

"Who were you talking to?"

"That was Stacy."

"Your roommate?"

"Yes."

"Why were you calling her *babe?* What's going on, Heather?"

"I've been meaning to tell you this for a while, but Stacy isn't just my roommate. She's my…my…girl-friend."

"Yeah, I know she's your friend."

"No…Stacy is also my lover."

"Lover?" Dash's eyes widened. "When…when did you turn gay?" he'd asked in total disbelief.

"I've always been bisexual, Dash. I…"

He cut her off. "Heather, why are you with me if you're into women? Has this entire time we've been together been a lie?" Dash stood silent for a moment as the news of his girlfriend's true sexual identity sank in.

Heather stepped closer to Dash, but he moved back. "No, it hasn't been a lie. I love you, Dash."

"Apparently you love Stacy, too."

"The truth of the matter is I want to be in a relationship with both of you. Stacy and I have discussed it, and we want you to join us in a polyamorous relationship."

"A poly…what?"

"A polyamorous relationship is a committed relationship between multiple people," she explained.

"Look, Heather, I'm not into threesomes."

"It's not a freaky ménage à trois. Our relationship would be exclusive, exactly like a regular relationship, except with three people instead of two. I really think it could work. Whenever the three of us are together we always have so much fun. Remember the time we ordered in pepperoni pizza and watched that sci-fi movie from the eighties? We all laughed so hard at the bad special effects that our sides hurt. Remember?"

"Of course I remember. What does that have to do with anything? Watching a movie together is a far cry from having a relationship."

"I was just reminding you how well we get along. To warm up to the idea, we could start out slow by going on a date with Stacy," she had said, trying to sway him.

"I don't think so. Sorry, but that's not for me. Heather, you should have told me the truth about your sexuality and let me make the choice whether or not I wanted to be with someone who is bisexual. Instead, you made the choice for me." Dash was hurt and a bit confused. Heather had never let on that she was also sleeping with a woman. Now it totally made sense why Heather and Stacy had only a one-bedroom apartment. Heather had told Dash that Stacy slept in the living room on the pullout sofa. Looking back now, he realized that was obviously a lie.

Dash didn't have a problem with homosexuality. As far as he was concerned, whom a person slept with was their business. He just chose to sleep with one woman at a time.

"I'm sorry, Dash, for not telling you sooner."

"So am I," he had said with disappointment in his voice.

"Don't let this interfere with what you and I have. I truly love you, Dash. Although I was hoping the three of us could have a relationship, I'll be content with just you and I."

"I don't think so, Heather. I wouldn't want you to resent me later. You should be able to have the type of relationship you desire."

Heather had moved closer to Dash, and this time he didn't shy away. They hugged for one last time.

"I wish you the best, Heather."

After Heather's true confession, he'd cut their vacation short. Dash had planned to take her for a gondola ride in Venice and propose, which of course had never happened. Dash hadn't spoken to Heather since they'd returned to New York over a year ago.

"Hey, man, you look deep in thought," Vance said, approaching his friend.

"I was thinking about Heather."

"Instead of breaking up with her, you should have invited her roommate to join you guys in Italy. Now, that would have been a trip to remember," Vance said, chuckling.

"I don't like sharing my woman or my body." Dash had grown up in a religious family with good moral values, values he'd carried over into adulthood.

"You're a better man than I am. I for one would have enjoyed both women...together and separately."

"I'm sure you would have."

Growing up, Vance had always been more adventurous than Dash. Vance's parents were extremely liberal and had allowed their children to explore and express their imagination.

As they were talking, the older gentleman and the redhead staggered out of the bar arm in arm. Vance took a seat next to Dash.

"So...congratulations on the new gig."

"Thanks, but it's not official yet."

"I got your message, and I'll be happy to look over the contract. But why are you going to work for another company when your family has a multimillion-dollar textile business in Italy? You could move there and live a life of luxury. You could have the plant manager do all the heavy lifting, so you could work a few days a week and play the rest of the time."

"I'm not ready to kick back just yet. Don't get me wrong—I'm grateful for the opportunities my family's wealth has afforded me. My grandfather started that company with nothing and made it into a thriving busi-

ness. I want to do the same with my designs. I don't want
to ride on the coattails of my family's success—I want
to make my own mark on the world of fashion."

Dash was tired of people thinking all he had to offer
were his good looks. He was well educated and had
a natural gift for designing clothes, jewelry and even
handbags.

"That's admirable of you, man. Most people in your
position would relax and enjoy the spoils."

Dash and Vance had been best friends since high
school. They had been the stars of the school's soccer
team and had remained close friends after graduating.

"Excuse me, but those two women at the end of the
bar would like to buy you guys a drink," the bartender
said.

Dash peered down the bar and saw two attractive
women, both dressed in tight black dresses that exposed way too much cleavage and both wearing heavy
makeup. The ladies were exposing nearly all of their
teeth and indelicately waving their arms.

"I'll take a pass," he said. Dash had spent more than
enough time drinking with random women and was
ready to find that special someone to settle down with.

"Come on, man. Don't be a party pooper. They look
eager and willing to please," Vance said as he waved
back to the duo.

Dash and Vance had that "wow" effect on women.
They were both handsome in their own way. While
Dash had olive skin and curly hair, Vance's complexion
was dark, nearly chocolate, and he wore his hair closely
shaven. Whenever the two were together, women approached them as if they were rock stars.

"Vance, don't let me stop you." Dash went into his

bag, took out a folder and handed it to his friend. "Here's the contract."

"I'll look it over first thing in the morning and get back to you."

"Thanks. I'm going to call it a night."

"You sure?" Vance stuck the folder in his briefcase and then glanced down the bar at the two women. "They are gorgeous. Come on—just have one drink with us."

"No, thanks, but knock yourself out. Hey, maybe you'll have that threesome you've always dreamed about," Dash said, getting up from the bar stool.

"Here's hoping!" Vance said, making his way toward the women.

As Dash walked down Fifth Avenue on his way home, his mind drifted back to Lark. He had read about her professional life online, but all he had learned about her personal life was that she was single. There hadn't been any mention of Lark being involved in a relationship—past or present. There hadn't even been any pictures of her in a social setting. He smiled at the possibility of dating Lark.

Man, keep your mind on business. She's your new boss, not your new girlfriend.

With that thought in his mind, he shifted focus and began thinking about the new and exciting clothing he was going to design for Randolph on the Runway, whether he was dating his boss or not.

Chapter 4

Dash's background check had come back clean and Lark was eager for him to start. Not only to see what designs he was going to come up with for the new collection, but to also get another gander at the strikingly good-looking younger man. Although she had no plans of ever dating her new hire, she saw no harm in letting herself look.

Today was to be Dash's first day. After her early workout at the gym, Lark had taken a little extra time that morning getting ready. She wore a feminine floral dress with prints of pink and orange blossoms that she'd designed herself. A thin green belt cinched her slim waist and her bob-length hair, left loose, framed her face perfectly. She finished the look with a pair of mint-green, pointy pumps. Lark's lips were stained with her signature blood-orange glossy lipstick, and she wore a hint of perfume.

Lark was sitting at her drawing table in her large corner office, working on a sketch for the new spring/summer collection. She had come into the office early to get a jump on the designs before her duties as COO took over her day. Lark was busy putting the finishing touches on a drawing when she heard someone knock. She looked up and smiled slightly.

"Good morning. You're here early," she said.

"I have some ideas in my head that I want to get down on paper. You're here early, too. You must have had the same thought," Dash said from the doorway.

Lark took in his physique as he stood there looking like a modern-day Adonis. He wore a baby-blue skinny-leg suit that fit his body to perfection with a crisp, stark white shirt and a pink tie. His look was professional, with an artsy edge. Lark had always prided herself on her style of dress, but now with Dash on her team, she would have to step up her game.

"Yes. I've already started sketching for the new line."

"Let me see what you're working on," he said, walking over to her drawing table.

Dash was standing so close to Lark that she could smell his cologne. She took a soft whiff and inhaled base notes of bergamot, jasmine and vanilla.

He smells good enough to eat, she thought.

"I like the leg of the pant. It fits the ankle nicely. But what about dropping the crotch half an inch? Do you mind?" Dash asked, picking a pencil up from the drawing table.

"Go for it." Lark moved back so he could have easier access to the sketchbook. As he drew, Lark stared at his strong hands and imagined his long, lean fingers caressing her skin.

Dash made the quick adjustment to the drawing. "What do you think?"

Lark peered down at what he had done and nodded her head. "Wow, moving the crotch down a bit makes a huge difference. Now the pants have more movement."

"I'm going to like working here. We're going to make an awesome team," he said.

Lark looked up into his face and found herself mesmerized by his bright smile. A few seconds passed before she glanced away. Lark was determined to keep her mind on business and not get lost in the younger man's charm.

"Did you bring the contract?" she asked.

Dash opened his messenger bag and took out a folder. "Here you go, signed and delivered."

Lark took the folder and placed it on the drawing table. "Did you have an attorney look over the contract so you know what you're signing up for?" Lark didn't want a replay of what she had experienced with Sebastian.

"Yes, I did, and he pointed out the proprietary clause."

"You do understand that everything you design for Randolph on the Runway is the property of the company?"

"Of course."

"And you don't have a problem with that?" she asked.

"No, not at all. My creativity is endless, and while I'm here, I plan to give you a hundred and ten percent."

"Great. That's what I want to hear. Now let me give you the dime tour and show you to your office."

Employees had started to arrive and settle in as Lark and Dash made their way across the opposite end of the floor. The loft offices of Randolph on the Runway had been redesigned by Lark, who had worked closely with an architect to create an inviting environment. The former outdated space had been dark and cramped. The renovated offices were now hip and chic, with cream leather seating and sleek teak furniture. There was colorful abstract artwork on the exposed-brick walls. The interior offices, framed in floor-to-ceiling plate glass, were visible from the corridors, giving the entire space an open and airy feel.

"This is our kitchen. The refrigerator is stocked with water, sandwiches, salads and healthy snacks. There's a single-cup coffee machine, which also makes tea. This drawer," she said, pulling out a drawer to her left, "is filled with take-out menus from nearby restaurants."

"That's good to know. Sometimes when I'm working, I don't want to interrupt my flow by going out to lunch."

"I know what you mean. Sometimes when I'm on a roll I can work straight through lunch. Come on—let me show you the rest of the space."

Lark led the way out of the small kitchen and continued down the hall. She stopped in front of a closed door, opened it, stepped inside and turned on the lights. "This is the showroom."

"I love the exposed-brick walls and vaulted ceiling."

"Thank you. I had the entire space redesigned. I wanted a loft-type atmosphere. This is where we keep our collections, meet with buyers and fit models for upcoming shows."

Dash went over to a rack of clothing and browsed through the items. He pulled out a dress. "This gown reminds me of the dresses they wore in the forties. The rose taffeta material looks authentic. What happened to the seams?" he asked, holding the ripped gown.

"It's a long story that I'd rather not retell. But I'm

glad you like the dress. It's one of my designs." Lark was pleased that Dash had commented on the gown. She knew her instincts about the dress had been right all along and it felt good to be validated by the young designer.

"You're quite talented."

Lark felt herself blushing as if she were the new hire and he were her boss. "Thank you. Let me show you to your office before my morning meeting." She turned off the lights and walked out with Dash following closely behind.

"This is your office," Lark said, entering a well-appointed room. The space was almost identical to Lark's, but smaller, with a teak desk, drawing table and sitting area. "The junior designers who'll be working under your supervision sit out here," she said, stepping back through the doorway and gesturing toward four cubicles.

As she was talking, a short, shapely brunette dressed in cargo pants and a T-shirt and wearing shades approached them. "Good morning, Ms. Randolph."

"Hi, Jessica. Let me introduce you to Dash Migilio, our new lead designer. You'll be reporting directly to him as stated in the email that Angelica sent out."

Jessica lifted her sunglasses and stared at Dash. "I'm really going to love coming to work now," she mumbled.

"Excuse me?" Lark asked.

"Oh, nothing." Jessica moved closer to Dash and extended her hand. "So very nice to meet you, Dash. Or should I call you Mr. Migilio?" she said, batting her eyes.

"Nice to meet you, too, Jessica. Dash is fine."

"You sure are," Jessica said, loud enough for everyone to hear.

Lark gave Jessica a disapproving look. "Jessica, if you're going to have a problem working with the new lead designer, I'll be happy to move you over to Aisha's team," Lark said sternly.

"No need, Ms. Randolph. I won't have a problem working with Mr. Migilio," Jessica said, changing her tune.

"Jessica, when you get a chance, let me see what you've been working on," Dash said.

"Sure," Jessica responded. She made her way to her cubicle, but not before turning around and giving Dash another appraising once-over.

Jessica's lustful glance didn't go unnoticed by Lark. She was going to admonish the young designer, but Lark really couldn't blame Jessica for staring at Dash. He was without a doubt worthy of a second and even a third look.

Once Jessica was out of earshot, Lark turned to Dash and said, "I like the way you handled that."

"What?" he asked.

"The way you ignored Jessica's not-so-subtle innuendos. You acted as if she weren't drooling all over you."

"Lark, I'm a professional. I don't mix business with pleasure. My personal life is just that…personal."

"Good to hear, because I think she's developing a crush on you. I can move her over to the other team if need be."

"Trust me. I can handle Jessica and any other employee who tries to make an inappropriate advance."

Does that include me? Lark wanted to say, but of course she didn't. She knew she had to stop thinking of Dash in a lustful way. He had been hired to do a job, and unfortunately, that job didn't include seducing the boss.

Chapter 5

Lark was meeting her best friend, Darcy McCay, at a day spa in Union Square for an afternoon of relaxation and pampering. Lark and Darcy's relationship had started off a bit rough when they'd first met at Randolph on the Runway. Lark had moved up from the drafting department, where she had worked for six months learning the art of pattern design. Lark's grandfather felt she had spent enough time in that part of the company and had promoted her to the ready-to-wear division to study under Darcy, a senior designer. Darcy was a few years older than Lark and was eager to teach the ingenue, but Lark proved to be quite a challenge. Instead of soaking up the information Darcy was dispensing, Lark had her own opinions about how the line should be designed.

"Instead of putting the split in the back, why don't we place it off center?" Lark had said.

"No, I like the split right where it is," Darcy had replied.

"Most designers place the split in the back. Don't you want to stand out?"

Darcy had looked up from her sketchbook. "Excuse me?"

"Don't you want to make your mark on the industry?"

"I have made my mark. The inside-out jumpsuit I designed won the Council of Fashion Designers Award a few years ago." Darcy's voice had been filled with pride.

"I remember seeing that jumpsuit in the trades. It was so unique and different. I had no idea you won a CFDA. Congratulations. But I still believe the split should be moved."

"I realize this is your family's company, but I'm currently your boss, and the final decision is mine. Your grandfather sent you to my division so I could take you under my wing. Please do us both a favor and learn what I'm trying to teach you."

From that day on, Lark did more listening than talking, and as a result she gained a wealth of knowledge from the senior designer, not only about the business of fashion, but about life. Lark had always been mature for her age. She hadn't gone out binge drinking like most of her college classmates had. She'd preferred hanging out with Darcy whenever she had spare time. They would dine at four-star restaurants, go to fashion industry events and relax at Darcy's summer home in the Hamptons. Darcy would school Lark on nuances of men, teaching her to not act eager and desperate when a man was interested. Darcy had told Lark that men were hunters, and that they liked the art of the chase.

Lark was an only child, and she thought of Darcy as an older sister and willingly took her advice.

Darcy eventually left Randolph on the Runway to start her own design firm, but she and Lark had remained close.

Lark arrived first. She had never been to the trendy spa and glanced around at the zebra rugs and modern decor.

"Welcome to Brigitte Mansfield European Day Spa," the receptionist said.

Before Lark could respond, Darcy rushed into the spa. "Sorry I'm late…" Darcy said. She was tall and thin as a reed. She had bronze skin and long, honey-blond hair. Before becoming a designer, Darcy had been a teen model. She was dressed in a sleek, cream-colored sheath and gold gladiator sandals.

Lark hugged her friend. "Hi there."

Darcy air-kissed Lark. "How are you, sweetie?"

"Good. Just a bit stressed."

"Well, that's why we're here. I promise you, after our spa day, we'll feel as good as new. The masseuses here have magic fingers."

"Right this way, ladies," the receptionist said, leading them toward the back.

After Lark and Darcy had changed into terry-cloth robes, they were shown to a private area where they each had the spa's signature facial.

"Hmm, this mask smells delectable," Lark commented.

"That's because it's made with cranberries, truffle oil and almonds. I get this facial on a regular basis. This mask really helps to ward away those unsightly frown lines."

Once their faces had been treated with tender loving care, they went into another room to get massages. They lay facedown on the table and let the masseuses work their magic. Lark closed her eyes and let her mind drift as the tension in her shoulders was kneaded away. The masseuse's hands gliding over her skin felt wonderful. Suddenly, Lark's thoughts shifted to Dash.

I wonder if he gives good massages.

Lark could picture Dash naked, drizzling oil on her skin, straddling her backside and rubbing his masculine hands up and down her back, caressing her tired muscles. After he had finished with her backside, she would turn over and let him smear the oil all over her breasts. She smiled at the thought of Dash taking her nipples between his fingers and rubbing them until they hardened. He would then admire her beckoning breasts, lean down and ever so gently lick and suck her nipples. Lark imagined Dash getting so turned on by her that his manhood would grow inch by inch until he was swollen with desire. He would then rub the head of his penis against the inside of her thigh and work his way up to her G-spot. Before slipping on a condom, Dash would tease her clit with his manhood until she was on the verge of coming. Lark's face would twist with pleasure and then she would cry out the words *Make love to me!* They would take turns pleasing each other all night, until the bottle of massage oil was empty and their bodies were spent from hours of making love. Only then would they drift off into a well-earned slumber.

"Didn't I tell you the masseuses here are amazing," Darcy said, interrupting Lark's naughty little daydream.

"I'm sorry. What did you say?"

"Were you asleep? I don't blame you. This massage will definitely lull you into total relaxation."

"Yes, among other things…"

After a few hours of being pampered like queens, Lark and Darcy left the spa feeling like a million bucks. They headed over to a Brazilian restaurant that had legendarily fresh cuisine and potent caipirinhas.

"Word on the street is that Sebastian quit RR and has started his own design firm. I understand he's ramping up production to debut his line at the spring/summer show," Darcy said once they were seated.

"Really? Is that so?"

"Yes, it's all over the fashion blogs. He's really ramping up a word-of-mouth buzz about his new collection."

"Sebastian might talk a good game. However, I seriously doubt his line will be ready in time for the spring/ summer show. And anyway, he's lying about quitting RR. He didn't leave on his own will. I fired him."

"Oh, that's news to me. Why did you let him go? When I interviewed Sebastian as my replacement, I thought he was a good fit for Randolph on the Runway."

"He was, until he started getting arrogant and out of control. I hadn't planned on letting him go, but he had no respect for me as his boss," Lark told her and then recounted the story of how Sebastian nearly destroyed one of her designs.

"Oh, a bit like you were when you first started working with me, minus ripping one of the pieces," Darcy said with a chuckle.

"Was I that bad?" Lark asked, sounding ashamed.

"Nothing I couldn't handle. After you checked your attitude at the door, we got along perfectly."

As they were talking the waiter came over. "Are you ready to order, ladies?"

"I'll have the coconut shrimp with the mango salsa," Lark responded.

"What's better—the roasted chicken with plantains or the beer-battered fish?" Darcy asked.

"They're both yummy. Personally, I prefer the beer-battered fish," the waiter responded.

"Okay, fish it is."

After the waiter left the table, Lark continued.

"Thanks again for having patience with me, Darcy. You really taught me a lot."

"You were a quick study. Have you hired another lead designer?"

Lark's mouth formed into a slight smile. "I have. His name is Dash Migilio."

"What's that smirk for?" Darcy asked, noticing the expression on her friend's face.

"Just thinking about him makes me smile. Not only is Dash talented, but he's gorgeous. He's Italian-American with a handsome face and killer body. You should see the way his suits fit—it's as if they were sculpted to his body. And he's extremely talented."

"Sounds like you have a major crush."

Lark thought for a moment. "I guess I do. But of course I haven't let on that my heart beats a little faster when I'm around him. See, that's another thing you taught me—to act cool and collected around attractive men."

"It might be hard to maintain control sometimes, but the more aloof you act, the more they'll want you. Good-looking guys aren't used to women ignoring them. They're accustomed to ladies throwing themselves at their feet. Is he married?"

"No, but I think he has a girlfriend. I saw a picture on his tablet of him and a beautiful blonde cozied up on a beach. They seemed really happy."

"Well, that's probably for the best. A relationship with a coworker can be a slippery slope. When the relationship is going good, work can be heaven, but after the breakup…and there's usually a breakup, coming to work can seem like a nightmare. Trust me, I know. I've had my share of work relationships gone awry."

"You're right, and that's why I'm keeping my feelings to myself. Dash will never know how I feel. Besides, its just a little crush, which will soon fade away."

Although Lark spoke the words, she had an inkling that her feelings for the young designer were more than a crush. A part of Lark was glad that Dash wasn't available; she needed to stay focused on developing the new collection. However, another part of her wanted nothing more than to make her daydream of making love to Dash a reality.

Chapter 6

Dash had settled into his new position as lead designer with full confidence and had taken charge of his team as if he had been with the company for years. Within a few days of starting, he had met with his team of four to present his vision for the new collection. He then reviewed their work individually and quickly assessed their strengths and weaknesses. Jessica had the most talent out of all her counterparts. Her designs were cutting-edge and out of the box. Dash had been reluctant to shower her with too much praise. He didn't want Jessica to get the wrong idea. Dash had no romantic interest in the younger designer.

Although he was still in his twenties, Dash was mature beyond his years and a seasoned businessman. Having spent many summers working in his family's textile mill, and learning every aspect of the business, Dash knew how to manage employees effectively. He could also design unique fabrics, clothing and accessories.

Late in the day, Dash sat in his office at the drawing table. He had attached his phone to mini speakers and the soft sounds of Michael Franks flooded his office. Dash was working on a leisure suit for the new line. He was in a zone, wielding a pencil and sketching feverishly. His shirt's sleeves were rolled up to his elbows, exposing dark hair on his forearms.

"Excuse me," Jessica said, standing in the doorway.

Dash swiveled around on the padded stool. "Hey, Jessica, what's up?"

"Some of us are going out for drinks after work to celebrate Aisha's birthday. You wanna come?"

"No, thanks. I'm on a roll designing a piece for the new collection and will be working late tonight."

"Oh, okay. Well…if you want, I can skip the party and stick around in case you need any help."

Dash gave Jessica an appraising look. She had on a sexy black dress that hugged her ample breasts and full hips. Dash noticed she had been coming to work lately wearing provocative clothing, no doubt trying to seduce him. It wasn't working. Jessica was attractive, but Dash had no interest in pursuing her on a personal basis. To him, she was just another employee, no matter how sexily she dressed.

Dash watched as Jessica's gaze traveled down to his crotch area. He closed his legs, ending her peep show. "No, that won't be necessary. Go out and have fun. I'll see you tomorrow."

"Thanks. I'll try. Are you sure you don't need me?"

"Positive."

"Good night, Dash."

"Good night."

Once Jessica was gone, Dash turned his attention back to the sketch pad in front of him. He rendered three different versions of the suit within two hours. He wanted to give Lark a variety to choose from. One suit had slim pencil-leg pants with a long blazer, the second suit had cropped pants with a waist jacket and the third had full palazzo pants with a bolero jacket. By the time he'd finished working, it was well after hours and most of the employees had gone for the day.

Dash stood and stretched. He had been sitting so long that his limbs had grown stiff. He hadn't eaten since lunch and his stomach was beginning to growl with hunger pains. He tucked the pencil behind his ear, left his office and headed down the hall to the company canteen. The automatic lights flickered on as he stepped inside. The small kitchen was well-appointed, with black marble countertops, stainless-steel appliances, a gourmet coffee machine, a high-powered juicer and small café-type tables and chairs.

One of the things Dash loved about working at Randolph on the Runway—aside from seeing Lark daily—was the fully stocked kitchen. He took a knife-and-fork packet out of one of the drawers, opened the fridge, reached for a prepackaged Cobb salad and a bottle of water and sat at one of the small tables. He opened the lid on the container, ripped the cellophane from the plastic utensils and began chowing down.

"I see I'm not the only one burning the midnight oil," Lark commented, coming into the room.

Dash stopped chewing midbite and eyed Lark. She had been in meetings the entire day and he hadn't seen her since yesterday. Dash admired her outfit. She wore a tailored navy-and-white-striped shirtdress with a beige belt clenching her waist and a pair of pointy beige sling-back pumps. Her hair was tucked behind her ears and her lips were stained with reddish-orange lipstick.

I wonder if her lips taste as good as they look was the first thing that popped into his mind. Dash exhaled and said, "I just finished sketching three variations of a suit for the new line. I was on a roll and didn't want to break the momentum by stopping to eat."

"I know what you mean. It's hard to stop when the ideas are flowing."

Lark went over to the coffeemaker, popped a tiny pod of hazelnut-flavored coffee in the machine, put her mug underneath the spout and waited for the liquid to brew. Once the steaming hot coffee filled her cup, she went over to where Dash was sitting and took a seat beside him.

"I'd love to see what you're working on. I've also sketched a couple of dresses that I want to include in the collection."

"I'll show you my sketches if you show me yours," Dash said with a flirtatious smile.

"Deal… So how's your first week going? I've been meaning to stop by your office all week, but I've been putting out fires left and right."

Dash studied her face as she spoke. He noticed a frown line creasing her brow. "Is there anything I can help with?"

She took a sip of coffee and then said, "Not really."

"You seem stressed. What's the matter?" he asked with concern in his voice.

"One of my suppliers is going out of business. I just got the word this morning. I've worked with this company for years and love their craftsmanship. I've spent all day on the phone trying to find a replacement, but none of the companies I've talked with so far can deliver the goods in time for production of the new line."

"What type of supplier are you looking for?"

"A textile mill, but not just any factory. I need one capable of producing a custom line of silk fabrics. I've designed new patterns that will help us stand out from the rest."

Dash's face lit up like the lights in Times Square, and he began smiling from ear to ear.

"What are you grinning about? This isn't funny. If I can't find a textile mill fast, I'll have to scrap my plans to use the new fabric designs for the spring/summer line."

"Problem solved!" Dash said, nearly blurting out the words.

"Excuse me?"

"Have you forgotten my family owns a textile mill in Italy?"

Lark's eyes widened. "Oh…that's right! I've been so busy lately working on the details for the new collection that it totally slipped my mind that I have a possible resource right under my nose."

"You most certainly do."

"What's the name of your family's company?"

"Migilio il Tessuti."

"What's the likelihood of Migilio il Tessuti being able to produce custom bolts of silk fabric in a short amount of time?"

"Very good. I know the owners!"

"Seriously, Dash, do you think the mill can manufacture what we need?"

"Of course they can. Even though I'm in New York,

I'm in constant touch with the mill. The plant manager has told me things have been slow lately. They won't be backed up with orders, so they can start production as soon as possible."

"That's great news! Come back to my office and I'll show you the fabric designs."

Dash abandoned his salad and followed Lark out of the kitchen. As she walked ahead of him, he checked out her rear view. She swayed sensuously. Her hips moved smoothly against the fabric of the dress, and the backs of her calves were firm and tight. Dash inhaled the aroma of her perfume straight into his nostrils. He noticed that it was the same fragrance she wore the other day and he found it deliciously enticing. He took another whiff before they reached her office.

Lark crossed the threshold and went to her desk. Sitting atop a pile of papers was her sketch pad. She flipped it open and handed the pad to Dash.

"Here are the fabric designs. What do you think?"

Dash studied the drawings and then said, "These are fantastic. I love the use of tone-on-tone overlays, and the color combinations of peach, coral and teal are spot-on for spring/summer."

"Thanks. Do you think the mill can re-create my designs?"

"I'm positive it won't be a problem. The mill has a rich history of producing fabrics for royalty, so your designs will be in good hands," Dash said, reassuring Lark.

"How soon can we go into production?"

"As soon as we book a flight to Italy and meet with the plant manager. We'll need to go there in person, show him the drawings and have a sample run made before production starts."

"Dash, I don't think I'll be able to get away. The accessories division is running behind schedule. Orders are still coming in from the last show and I need to finish the new sketches."

"Lark, do you trust your division heads?"

"Of course I do."

"Then you have to delegate. We'll only be in Italy long enough to oversee the sample run and then we'll be on a plane back to New York. We shouldn't be gone longer than a week."

Lark exhaled. "Sometimes I do have a hard time letting go of responsibilities. Every division of the company is near and dear to my heart. I guess some might call me a control freak. It's just that I want every aspect of the new collection to be flawless. The competition in this industry is fierce, and we can't afford to lose any market share."

"I understand. That's all the more reason to go and oversee the samples. Besides, it's not like you're going away on vacation. It's work-related. We won't be away from the office for too long," Dash said.

"You're right. What am I thinking? This is important. The new fabrics will definitely give us an edge."

"I'll make all the arrangements and will call the plant manager to give him a heads-up."

"Thanks, Dash."

"Don't mention it. I'm here to make the line the best it can be, and if that means going to Italy to manufacture custom bolts of fabric, then that's what we'll do."

"I truly appreciate your help."

"I'll email you with the details, once I secure our plans."

"Why don't I have Angelica make the reservations?"

"Don't get me wrong—I think your assistant is extremely efficient, but Florence is my second home and I can handle the details with my eyes closed."

"Okay, sounds good."

Dash moved with purpose back to his office. Excitement began to fill his spirit at the thought of showing Lark the countryside of Florence and his family's business. He hadn't brought a woman to Italy since Heather, and he welcomed the female company. Although their visit would be brief, Dash planned to make the most of their time in Italy.

Chapter 7

True to his word, Dash had handled the arrangements for their trip to Florence. He'd booked the hotel and airline tickets. Dash had even arranged for a car to pick her up from her apartment. All Lark had had to do was pack her bags and meet him at the airport. Their evening flight had been uneventful, with them both catching a little shut-eye on the plane, resting from a long week of work.

The morning sun beamed through the airplane's window, disturbing Lark's sleep. She blinked and peered around the first-class cabin. Dash wasn't in his seat adjacent to hers, and she breathed a sigh of relief. She didn't want him to see her unwashed morning face. Lark unbuckled the seat belt, reached underneath the seat in front of her to retrieve her overnight tote and made her way to the lavatory.

Inside the small space, she took a hand towel out of her tote, washed her face and freshened up. She changed clothes, replacing her jogging suit with a khaki pant-suit, a white sleeveless blouse and a pair of tan loafers. She combed her hair and touched up her makeup. Lark took in her reflection in the mirror. *Now I'm ready to be seen.* She tucked her hair behind her ears before un-latching the door.

"Wow, you look like you're ready to hit the ground running," Dash remarked once she reached their seats.

Lark moved past him and sat down. "For the sake of time, I thought we'd go directly to the mill and get started on the samples. I don't want to waste any time. I need to get back to New York as soon as possible. We can check in to the hotel afterward."

"Sounds good." Dash handed Lark a small tray. "The flight attendant came by when you were in the lavatory and I got you a cappuccino and a chocolate *cornetto.*"

He's so sweet! Lark thought as she reached for the tray. "Thanks." She took a sip. "Mmm, that's really good cappuccino."

"Yes, it is, isn't it? Try the *cornetto.* It's the Italian version of a croissant."

Lark took a bite of the buttery roll. "This is divine. I love Italian food, but I'll have to watch my calorie in-take while I'm here. Otherwise I'll bring home a few extra pounds."

"You don't have anything to worry about. You're perfect just the way you are."

He knows exactly what to say. Not only was Lark at-tracted to him physically, but she was discovering that Dash had a kind and giving spirit. His interior was just as beautiful as his exterior, and the combination was an aphrodisiac.

By the time they finished with their light Italian breakfast, the pilot announced their descent into Florence. Lark peered out of the window at the aerial view of the ancient city below, with its cluster of rustic clay tile rooftops and winding narrow streets.

After going through customs, they made a swift exit since neither had checked any luggage. Dash had hired a car and driver, who was waiting curbside to take them to the mill.

"After you," Dash said, taking Lark's tote out of her hand and helping her into the backseat.

"Thanks." Lark watched as he carried her bag around to the back of the mustard-colored four-door convertible. Dash wore jeans and a short-sleeved shirt that accentuated his biceps. Lark quickly imagined his arms embracing her in a tender hug and drawing her in close. Lark shook her head, trying to dismiss the thought. She was in Italy to conduct business, not to have a romantic rendezvous with a hot young designer.

Once Dash settled into the backseat next to Lark, he instructed the driver in Italian. Lark listened as his native language easily rolled off his tongue. In New York, Dash didn't speak with an accent, and Lark was surprised he was fluent in Italian. She was impressed and aroused as he spoke.

The car drove through the centuries-old town of Florence, the birthplace of the Renaissance—hometown of Michelangelo, Galileo and Leonardo da Vinci—passing such treasures as the Piazza del Duomo and the Palazzo Vecchio. Lark peered out of the window and marveled at the city's treasures. She had been to Italy numerous times, but she never tired of taking in its ancient architecture.

In no time, they were driving through the wrought-iron gates of Migilio il Tessuti. A tree-lined driveway led to a hewn-stone building that appeared as if it had been built centuries ago. The driver parked and they stepped out.

"This building is lovely," Lark said, standing in front of the entrance and gazing up at the structure.

"It was built in the eighteenth century. When my family bought the mill, they had the building refurnished but kept the integrity of the original design. The mill still has the original antique handlooms we use today."

"That's amazing. I can't wait to see them."

"Come on inside."

Dash led the way through the entrance of the mill, where they were greeted by Marco, the plant manager.

"*Benvenuta,* Signorina Randolph," Marco said in a thick Italian accent and extended his hand.

"Thanks so much for accommodating us on such short notice," Lark said as she shook his hand.

"*No problema.* Dash has told me about your dilemma. It is our pleasure to help in any way we can. This way." Marco gave Lark a tour of the facilities. "Most of our weavers are second- and third-generation artisans."

Although the factory had been renovated, it still had the original wooden columns and vaulted beams, giving it an antiquated feeling. Lark looked around and felt as if she had stepped back in time. She could just imagine families of nobility having their silk brocade garments constructed there. She noticed a strange-looking apparatus. "What's that?" she asked, walking over to the piece of equipment.

"It's a warping machine, and it's based on a design by da Vinci."

She ran her hand over the surface. "Does it work?"

"But of course," Marco responded.

"Our production process begins with hand-dyed, raw-spun Brazilian silk wound onto spools," Dash interjected. "Not only were fabrics for clothing made here back in the day, but textiles for palaces throughout Europe were crafted here, as well. Even though the mill is old, we've modernized the facilities to keep up with technological advances."

Lark was impressed by Dash's knowledge of the historic value of the mill. "It's good to know that Randolph on the Runway is in such esteemed company."

"Yes, the way we make fabrics has changed very little since the Renaissance," Marco said.

Lark reached into her tote, took out her sketch pad and handed it to Marco. "Here are the patterns I want to create."

Marco studied the drawings for a moment. "*No problema.* I'll submit your designs to our textile designer. We'll make strike-offs of your designs to make sure the color combinations are correct. You can come back tomorrow to give your approval."

"Awesome! Thank you so much."

"What time will the samples be ready?" Dash asked.

"You come back late afternoon. *Sì?*"

"*Sì. Grazie mille!*" Dash responded, thanking the plant manager.

"*Prego.*"

She shook Marco's hand and they made their way back to the car. Inside the car, Dash once again spoke to the driver in Italian before they drove off.

"Dash, thanks again for setting up the meeting with Marco. If you hadn't suggested your family's mill, I wouldn't have had time to find another resource to produce the custom silk for the new collection."

"Lark, you don't have to keep thanking me. I also have a vested interest in the success of the collection. After all, this will be the debut of my designs for RR."

"Guess you have a point. I'm hoping you'll get a positive review from the critics."

"No worries there. Although I'm young, you can rest assured I'll be the new King of Seventh Avenue!"

"I like your confidence."

Lark felt at ease. She leaned back on the seat and took in the Florentine countryside dotted with olive groves and lemon trees. When they reached the hotel, the first thing she noticed was the vine-covered chapel on the property, which looked as if it had been erected in the seventeenth century. Colorful flower beds adorned the exterior of the hotel, giving the building a welcoming feel.

Dash led the way into the hotel, which resembled an Italian villa, and went straight to the registration desk to check in.

"Here's your room key," he said, handing Lark a keycard. "Can I help you with your bag?"

"No, thanks. I've got it."

"Are you tired?" he asked as they walked to the bank of elevators.

"Not really. I'm too excited about seeing the sample run tomorrow."

"Why don't we go out to dinner? There's a quaint restaurant not too far from here."

"Sounds good."

"Let's meet in the lobby in an hour."

"Okay, perfect. That'll give me time to unpack and take a quick shower."

The elevator arrived and they stepped in. There was an awkward silence between them as they rode to their floor. Lark considered speaking, but she wasn't much for small talk.

When they reached her room, Lark stood in front of the door and fumbled with the key. She shifted the tote to her left hand.

"Here, let me help you," Dash said, taking the bag out of her hand.

Lark slipped the key into the slot and opened the door. She walked in with Dash following behind. Lark glanced around the antiques-furnished room and noticed a golden silk brocade bench at the end of the bed. "You can put the tote on the bench."

Dash had his back to her, and Lark watched him intently. He had a tight rear end and she found herself wondering what his body looked like in the buff. She had seen his hairy chest in the picture on his tablet, but in that photo, he was only partially nude.

"All right. See you in an hour." Dash headed to the door.

"Okay."

Once the door had shut behind him, Lark exhaled. She had to get a grip on her emotions. She wanted the young designer, but she was intent on keeping her feelings in check.

Chapter 8

Osteria delle Tre Panche was an old-world Italian restaurant not far from the center of town. Locals loved the quaintness as well as the delectable food of this tucked-away Florentine treasure, which was off the tourist track.

"I hope you don't mind sharing a table with other people," Dash said as they sat nearly elbow to elbow with another couple.

"No, not at all. I love the laid-back atmosphere." Lark glanced around. "It's extremely cozy. I can't believe there are only three benches in the entire place. It's a refreshing change from some of the cavernous restaurants in New York."

"Actually, *tre panche* translates to 'three benches,'" Dash told her.

"Well, that explains it."

"I hope you like truffles," Dash said, peering across

the wooden bench at Lark. He took in her sexy dress, which was made of black lace with a nude underlay. Dash imagined her wearing the dress without the slip underneath. He could picture the fabric accentuating her curves, her ample breasts poking through the lace. Dash couldn't stop himself from thinking about Lark. His attraction toward her only got stronger the more time they spent together.

"I love truffles."

"Good. We'll start with the beef tartare, foie gras and a bottle of wine. And then we'll have the white-truffle risotto and the cheese ravioli with shaved truffles."

"There goes my diet," Lark said with a chuckle.

Dash's eyes roamed her body. "Lark, trust me. You don't have anything to worry about. Even if you did gain a few pounds, you'd still be perfect."

Her cheeks blushed a rosy color. "Oh, come on. You have to say that… I'm the boss."

You can boss me around anytime, he thought. But what he said was "Since we're here, we have to order the osso buco. It's so tender and flavorful—the best I've ever eaten by far."

"That's just way too much food for two people."

"Don't worry. We'll space it out. We'll have wine, talk and *mangia.* Eat! Eat!" Dash said.

It may have indeed been too many dishes, but now that Dash had Lark all to himself, he wanted to relish their time together and not rush the evening.

After the waitress had brought the appetizers and a bottle of Lambrusco, they dug in. Neither had eaten anything since the in-flight meal and both were starving. Before long, they had polished off the foie gras and the beef tartare.

"Wow…that was delicious! I guess I was hungrier than I thought," Lark said, dabbing the sides of her mouth with a cloth napkin. She picked up her glass of wine and took a sip.

"The food here is orgasmic." Dash studied Lark's face and noticed her cheeks turning crimson once again.

"Yes, it is. So…I didn't know you were fluent in Italian."

"Even though I grew up in the States, I spoke Italian before I spoke English. My parents made sure I knew their native tongue, and I'm so glad they did. Being bilingual really comes in handy when dealing with Italian vendors."

"That's true. I'm actually thinking about taking a beginners' course. I've been meaning to do it for years, but have had too many things on my plate to take the time for a class."

"Forget about a class. I'll be happy to teach you."

"Oh, no, I wouldn't want to impose."

"It's not an imposition. As a matter of fact, we can start now… Say *buongiorno.*"

"Oh, that's an easy word. It means 'good morning.' *Banjurno,*" Lark said, pronouncing the word with an American accent.

"No, you have to form your mouth into an O shape," Dash instructed. "Now try it again."

"Banjurno," she repeated.

He reached across the table, took her chin in his hand and slightly pulled down, opening her mouth wide. Dash let his fingers linger on her soft skin. Touching her made the hairs on the back of his neck rise. "Now try it."

"Buon…giorno," Lark said, this time using the correct pronunciation.

He released her chin and clapped. "*Perfetto!* I think we're going to need more wine with our lesson." Dash refilled their glasses and touched his to Lark's. "*Salute—* Sah-loo-tay!"

"*Salute,*" she repeated, saying the word perfectly.

As the evening unfolded, they drank not one but two bottles of wine, during and after dinner. Two and a half hours later, they were completely satiated and slightly tipsy. When Dash pulled out his credit card to pay the bill, Lark objected.

"This is a business trip. You don't have to pay with your personal card unless you're going to expense the meal."

"I don't plan to get reimbursed for the pleasure of your company."

"Thank you. This was a lovely dinner. I'll definitely come back the next time I'm in Florence."

"You are more than welcome. I'm glad you enjoyed one of my favorite restaurants."

After the bill was paid, they moseyed out of the restaurant toward the waiting car, nearly leaning on each other. Their spirits were high.

"This was really fun!" Lark said with a lilt to her voice.

Dash opened the passenger door for her. "It sure was."

Once Lark settled in the backseat, she blurted out, "I'm not ready to go back yet. Let's go dancing."

"Dancing?" Dash asked, a bit surprised.

"Yep! I need to work some of this food off!"

Dash glanced over at Lark and noticed her tight office demeanor was completely gone, having been replaced with more of a free-spirit attitude, which he found welcoming. "Dancing it is."

He spoke to the driver in Italian and the car began winding through the narrow city streets. Before long, they pulled up in front of a popular nightclub for locals and tourists alike. The exterior of the club was abuzz with people impatiently standing behind the velvet rope, trying to gain entry.

Dash stepped out of the car, reached for Lark's hand and helped her out. He held her hand tightly as he made his way straight toward the entrance, not looking twice at the crowd of partygoers waiting in the long line.

"Dash, *buonasera!*" the doorman said with enthusiasm.

"*Buonasera,* Luigi. *Come stai?*"

"*Bene, bene!*"

The two men chatted in Italian for a few moments before converting back to English.

"What are you doing in town?"

"I'm here on business," Dash replied.

"Let's get together for a game of boccie before you leave."

"I'd love to, but this is a quick trip. Next time I'm in town, you've got yourself a match. I need to redeem myself from the last time you won," Dash said, chuckling.

"Deal!" Luigi hugged Dash, then stepped aside and let them in.

"Who was that?" Lark asked, yelling over the pulsating beat of the music.

"That's Marco's son. We've known each other since we were boys. His dad used to bring him to the mill during the summer and we would play boccie in the yard. Luigi used to beat me back then and he still does now."

Dash took hold of Lark's hand again and weaved his

way toward the dance floor. The club was buzzing with people gyrating to the rhythm of the DJ's pop music.

"Oh, I just love this song!" Lark started waving her arms in the air as she danced around, twirling her body as she moved.

Dash kept pace with her, all the while watching as her hips swayed to the music. The night had taken a completely different turn. Dash had had no idea they would wind up in the middle of a nightclub dance floor. Dash was seeing a completely different side of his boss and he loved the transformation.

"Would you like something to drink?" Dash asked once the song was over.

"No, thank you," she shouted. "I just want to dance. I haven't been out partying in so long that I almost forgot how good it feels to lose yourself in the music."

Dash watched as Lark closed her eyes and danced as if she were the only person on the dance floor. One song blended into the next as they kept pace with the beat. He wanted to pull her close, but didn't. Dash decided to follow Lark's lead. He wasn't going to assume that her dancing mood meant she was ready for a romantic rendezvous. At the moment he was content just being with his beautiful boss.

Chapter 9

Lark knew it wasn't the wine that had her in a joyous mood… It was Dash Migilio. He was proving himself to be everything she wanted in a man. Not only was he gorgeous, but he was smart, thoughtful, talented and accommodating. As she danced, Lark thought about Darcy's rule of maintaining control and not letting a man know you were interested. That philosophy had worked in the past, but Lark was still single and the years were quickly ticking by. She couldn't continue putting her biological clock on snooze if she wanted to have a family.

Lark opened her eyes and kept them on Dash as their bodies moved to the beat. The more she watched him, the more she realized how much she was falling for the young designer. Even though he was at least ten years younger than she, he was mature beyond his age. If Lark was ever going to find love, she would have to take a leap of faith and trust that Dash felt the same way.

Here goes, she thought as she danced closer and draped her arms around his neck. Lark searched his eyes, trying to get a read on him as she suggestively moved her body against his.

Dash didn't shy away. He took her by the waist and hugged her tightly.

Lark exhaled. She felt safe and secure within his arms and she let her inhibitions go. Although the beat of the music was fast, they began slow dancing to a rhythm of their own. Lark closed her eyes and rested her head on Dash's shoulder. She was so close to him she could smell the scent of his masculine cologne. Lark nuzzled her nose closer and took a deep breath. She then felt Dash's hand caressing the back of her head. He weaved his long fingers through her hair, gently massaging her scalp. His touch was relaxing and stimulating at the same time. Lark was quickly becoming aroused. Instinctively, her hips started to move against his groin.

Thoughts of doubt began crowding her mind. *What are you doing? He's your employee. He's too young for you. He's already taken.*

She took a step back. "I'm so sorry," she whispered in his ear.

"For what?"

"You have a girlfriend and I shouldn't make advances toward you."

Dash closed the gap between them, pulling her back into his embrace. "I'm not in a relationship. You can advance all you want."

"What about that picture I saw…?"

"On my tablet? That was my ex. What we shared is

long over. I'm free to be with whoever I want, and I want you."

Lark was elated to hear those words. Her leap of faith had proved not to be blind.

"Question," Dash yelled above the music. "Are you straight? I mean, you're not bisexual, are you?"

"Not at all! I'm only into men. I have no interest in women," Lark responded.

"Good. I'm not judgmental or anything. Whom a person sleeps with is their business. It's just that in the past I was left in the dark about certain things. Enough about that though."

Dash leaned in and introduced his mouth to hers. She didn't hesitate to return his kiss. Lark was oblivious to the people around them. The urgency she felt for him at that moment took precedence over any feelings of embarrassment. She could taste the wine on his lips. She was becoming intoxicated by his tongue as he explored her mouth. Lark's hips began grinding against him once again, searching for signs of excitement. She moved in even closer and felt his manhood tightening against her. She closed her eyes and held him tightly around the neck. Lark could feel the heat emanating from her body. She was on fire. The intensity between them was getting stronger by the second.

"Let's get out of here," Dash whispered in her ear, taking her by the hand.

He just read my mind, Lark thought, following closely behind Dash as he cut a path through the pulsating crowd of dancers.

Sexual tension continued to fill the air on the ride back to the hotel as they sat closely together in the backseat. Lark wanted so badly to straddle Dash and grind suggestively against him, but the driver was within mere inches of them. She secretly wished for a glass partition so they could continue with their heated foreplay. Lark looked over at Dash and bit her bottom lip. She was finding it difficult to control herself.

Dash touched her mouth and rubbed her lips with his finger. He then parted her lips and Lark began slowly sucking his index finger as if it were covered with honey. She quietly and slowly brought his long finger in and out of her mouth, being careful not to make any slurping sounds, all the while staring directly into his eyes.

Dash removed his finger and traced the outline of her lips. "I love your mouth. It's perfectly shaped."

Lark exhaled. "Thanks."

He leaned in and gently kissed her. "I couldn't help myself."

Lark mirrored his move by kissing his lips. "Neither could I."

They didn't exchange any more words—only lustful looks—until they were back at the hotel. They waltzed through the lobby and held hands as they waited for the elevator to arrive. Once the doors opened, they stepped into the empty car. Dash pressed the button for their floor and then pinned Lark against the mirrored wall, firmly pressing his body against hers.

Lark could feel the urgency in his pants as she rotated her hips, matching him move for move. She clung to him as they kissed passionately, hungry for one another.

The doors opened and they stumbled out, drunk with desire as they made their way down the hallway arm in arm. When they reached her door, Lark reached inside her purse and produced the keycard. She inserted the card into the slot and opened the door. She stepped inside, but Dash hesitated.

"I'll be right back," he said.

"Where are you going? I thought you... I mean...I thought we were..."

"Oh, don't worry—we are indeed! Stand right here and keep the door open. I'll be back in a sec."

Lark stood in the doorway and watched Dash quickly sprint down the corridor to his room. He went inside, and before she had time to cool off, he was running back to her.

"Thought we might need these," he said, holding up a few condoms between his thumb and index finger.

"Oh, yes, we will. Now get in here!"

"Whatever you say, boss lady."

"*Whatever,* huh? I like the sound of that."

Lark flipped on the lights and stepped inside as Dash made his way into the room, closing the door firmly behind him. She kicked off her shoes and slipped her dress over her head, leaving a trail of clothing as she made her way to the bed. Lark eased onto the king-size bed and leaned against the pillows, striking a pose in her low-cut bra and black lace thong.

Dash went to the nightstand and put down the condoms. He began unbuttoning his shirt, but stopped and stared at Lark. *"Molto bene!"*

"You like?"

"Very much. Like I've said before, you are simply perfect!"

Lark smiled and watched as Dash stripped down to his snug black boxer briefs. Her breath caught in her throat as she eyed his sculpted body. His pecs were well-defined. His abs rippled underneath his golden skin, and the bulge between his thighs was hard to ignore. He was indeed an Italian masterpiece, much like the statue of David.

She spread her legs and crooked her finger. "Get over here now!"

"Yes, boss lady."

Dash didn't hesitate. He crawled onto the bed like a panther en route to his prey.

Lark wrapped her arms around his neck, bringing him in closer. It had been way too long since she'd had a man in her bed, and Lark was well overdue for some heated lovemaking. She slowly moved her hands down the length of Dash's back, feeling the contours of his muscles. She stopped at his tight ass and began massaging his cheeks. Lark didn't stop until she felt him growing exponentially against her. She reached down and rubbed his engorged penis, feeling the outline of the bulbous head through his cotton underwear.

Dash rolled over to his side and slid off his boxers, unleashing his lethal weapon.

Lark stared at him with lustful eyes. "You're so big."

Dash took firm hold of his shaft and waved it at Lark. "And it's all for you." He then took a condom from the nightstand, tore the wrapper with his teeth and rolled the condom onto his manhood.

Lark watched impatiently. She could feel her juices flowing in anticipation of making love to him. She didn't have to wait long—Dash resumed his position, covering her body with his.

He held her leg to his waist and kissed her neck as he slowly and gently entered her. "You're so tight. Am I hurting you?"

"No, it feels good. Don't stop."

Dash continued inching into her and didn't stop until he was all the way inside. He picked up the pace, pumping deeper and deeper.

"Oh, yes… Dash… Yes…yes!" Lark closed her eyes and grinded back against him. Their rhythm caused the headboard to bump against the wall in Morse code–type taps. Lark interpreted each tap as saying, *Take me… Take me…now!* He was making such good love to her that a tear escaped her eye. Their connection was better than she could have ever imagined. Lark wanted to prolong their first time together, but she could feel her arousal increasing. She arched her back and moved her pelvis even closer to Dash. Their skin-to-skin gyrating was driving Lark wild. Her head thrashed back and forth on the pillow. She couldn't hold back any longer.

"I'm…coming…"

Before she reached the pinnacle, he stopped suddenly and pulled out.

"What are you doing? I was on the verge of…"

"Turn over," he said, his voice husky with lust.

Lark stared into his eyes and could see his want for her. She flipped over onto her stomach without questioning him. Dash was in control and she was enjoying every second of it.

He picked up where they'd left off. Dash held her hips, brought Lark to her knees and entered her from behind.

Lark bucked back against him as he eased his rod deeper and deeper into her wetness. She then moved her body in a circular motion, grinding against his hardness. Each passing second brought her closer and closer to the brink of ecstasy.

She leaned forward and bit into a pillow to keep from

screaming. This young man was rocking her world, bringing her into a state of ecstasy she had never experienced before.

"Does it feel good, baby?" Dash asked, lightly tapping her rear end with his hand.

"Yes…yes!"

Dash picked up the pace, making the headboard knock against the wall even louder.

Words escaped her as she surrendered to his manhood. Her body tensed and she eased down onto the bed as she came. She shuddered and trembled from the heated climax. Neither said a word. They lay silent in each other's arms with their eyes closed for a moment, enjoying the aftermath of their explosive, mind-blowing sex.

Chapter 10

After disposing of the condom, Dash rolled back into bed and eased under the covers next to Lark, who was staring up at the ceiling. She seemed to be in a daze. Dash put his arm around her shoulders and she rested her head in the crook of his arm.

"Are you all right?" he asked after a few minutes.

Lark sighed. "Oh, I'm better than all right… I'm fantastic! I never knew sex could be so good."

A broad smile lit up Dash's face. Pleasing her had been his sole objective, and from the exuberant lilt in her voice, he had done his job and then some. Dash wanted to be the only man Lark desired. He turned his head and kissed her on the cheek.

"There's much more where that came from. Tonight was just a prelude," he said with confidence.

"A prelude, huh? Aren't you the cocky one."

"I'm not cocky. I'm secure. I may be young, but trust and believe that I know how to make love to a seasoned woman like yourself."

"You surely do."

Dash watched Lark's face brighten with the afterglow of good sex. He hadn't expected the night to unfold as it had, but he was elated by the turn of events. Dash had often wondered what making love to Lark would be like. Now he didn't have to speculate any longer. The reality had been far better than the fantasy, and he wanted more.

Dash slipped his hand underneath the covers, down her taut stomach and between her legs. He peeled back the folds of her vulva and inserted a finger into her canal. She was still wet, and her moistness was turning him on. Dash plunged his finger in and out of her repeatedly, while fingering her clit with his index finger. He leaned up on his elbow, threw the covers back and increased the pace. Dash was digitally pleasing Lark and delighted in her pleasure.

She moaned, thrashing her head back and forth on the pillow.

He watched his finger going inside her and coming out covered with her juices. He switched fingers and licked his come-covered digit.

"You taste so good."

Lark didn't verbally respond, but her body was speaking volumes. She was arching her back and bucking like a young steer.

Dash didn't stop plunging until he heard her screaming...

"I'm coming. I'm coming! What...what...are...you doing to me?" she asked, her words coming out in spurts.

"I'm just making sure you're totally satisfied, that's all," he said, a wicked grin on his face.

"Oh, no worries there," she responded after she had recovered.

"Good. That's what I want to hear."

Lark curled over on her side and Dash moved behind her, holding her snugly around the waist. Dash closed his eyes and listened as Lark's breathing became more and more relaxed. Before long, they had drifted off to sleep.

Dash awoke with the sun, slipped out of bed, found his clothes on the floor and quickly dressed. He stood at the edge of the bed and watched Lark rest peacefully. He could have stared at her all morning, but he had moves to make. Dash eased the door open. He turned around, giving Lark one final look before leaving.

Back in his room, Dash arranged for the driver to pick him up, then showered and changed clothes. Before he and Lark returned to the mill later that day, Dash was planning an impromptu romantic lunch. They would be in Florence only a few days and he was anxious to show Lark his hometown.

The car was waiting out front. Dash hopped in and spoke to the driver in Italian, telling him the address of his family's estate, which wasn't too far from the hotel. Traffic was light at that time of the morning, and the car whizzed along until they entered the wrought-iron gates of Villa Migilio, a twenty-acre estate complete with an olive grove, lemon trees, an Olympic-sized swimming pool, tennis courts, an eight-hole golf course, a guest cottage and a pool cabana. The main house was a bone-colored, one-hundred-and-fifty-year-old, two-storied villa with a terra-cotta tile roof. Lush ivy wove its way down the south wall of the home, cascading like a green waterfall.

The car pulled up in the graveled circular driveway. Dash dismissed the driver for the day before stepping out and making his way inside. The foyer was tiled in ivory marble, and from the entrance he could see the grand staircase with an ornate gold banister, which led upstairs to six bedroom suites, each with their own balcony.

"Mama! Mama!" Dash yelled, as he walked through the living room with its opulent furnishings and artwork. His parents were art collectors, who had amassed a fortune in original oil paintings over the years.

"Dashie! What are you doing here?" A short, chubby woman came through the swinging kitchen door and embraced Dash in a bear hug.

"I have business at the mill. Where's Mama?"

"She's not here," Sophia, the housekeeper, told him.

Dash kissed the older woman on both of her rosy cheeks. Sophia had been with his family since he was a baby, and she was like an aunt to him. As a boy, he had even helped to teach her English. Whenever he was in town, Dash always spoke to Sophia in English, because he knew that she loved the practice. "Where is she?"

"She and your papa are in Capri on holiday."

"Oh? When did they leave?"

"Yesterday."

"How long will they be gone?"

"For ten days."

Dash's parents had retired to their Italian estate a few years ago, and they spent the majority of their time traveling. He usually spoke to his parents on a regular basis, but he had been busy lately and had been missing his weekly calls. He had yet to tell them about his new position. Dash had thought he'd get a chance to tell them during his visit.

"Guess I'll catch them next time. Sophia, I need your help."

"*Sì,* Dashie, whatever you want," she said. Sophia had a soft spot for Dash and had spoiled him all of his life.

"Come on. Let's go in the kitchen," he said.

Dash held open the swinging door to the kitchen, allowing Sophia to enter first. The interior of the villa had been gutted and renovated into a modern marvel. The chef's kitchen was equipped with a six-burner Bertazzoni range with bright red knobs and a double-door stainless-steel refrigerator. A professional espresso machine sat on the quartz countertop. The walls were painted a soothing pale yellow and the floors were covered with ceramic tile hand-painted in a geometric design.

"Sophia, I need to put together a picnic basket for lunch."

"Just for you?"

"No, I'll need enough food for two."

"Dashie, you have a lady friend?" Sophia asked, smiling.

"You could say that."

"Is Heather here? She was such a nice girl."

"Yes, she was, but Heather isn't with me. We're not together anymore."

Dash and Sophia shared a close relationship, and he had confided in her since he was a boy. Sophia had never had children, and she treated Dash more like a nephew than an employer.

"Oh, I'm sorry to hear that. Did you find another, love?"

Thinking about Lark made Dash smile. "I certainly hope so. She's a special lady and I want to prepare a special lunch for her. Can you help me put something delicious together?"

"*No problema!* I have some delicious treats for you and your lady friend."

Sophia went into work mode. She opened the refrigerator, took out prosciutto, a melon, a wedge of Pecorino Romano and a jar of homemade olive tapenade.

"I made tomato-basil focaccia yesterday," she said, reaching into the breadbasket on the counter.

"Hmm, sounds good. I'll be right back. I'm going to the wine cellar."

Dash crossed the floor, opened a door next to the pantry and went downstairs. The lower level of the villa included a billiards room, a walk-in humidor filled with hand-rolled cigars, a twelve-seat screening room and a fully stocked wine cellar. His parents loved to entertain whenever they were in town and kept the cellar stocked with a variety of champagne, wine and ports.

He went inside the cool exposed-brick cellar and perused the bottles of wine until he found the perfect vintage—a '97 Chianti and a pinot grigio made from local grapes. Dash was well schooled—from his parents—on the art of wines, learning at an early age which vineyards produced the best grapes and how the climate affected the crops. With his selections in hand, Dash trotted back upstairs.

"You like?" Sophia asked, presenting him with a perfectly packed wicker basket filled with delicious Italian delicacies.

Dash kissed her on the cheek. *"Grazie mille!"* he exclaimed.

Sophia responded, *"Prego!"*

"The only thing I need now is a blanket and then my picnic will be complete," he said, taking the basket in his arms.

"There's one in the front closet, folded on the top shelf."

"Thanks again, Sophia—you're the best! What would I do without you?"

"Oh, go on!" She blushed and shooed him out of the kitchen.

"I'll be back soon," he said. He made a beeline to the foyer and retrieved a green-white-and-red-checked blanket out of the closet before leaving.

His loafers made crunching sounds as he crossed the gravel driveway and entered a four-car garage a few feet away. Inside were luxury vehicles parked side by side—a vintage silver drop-top Aston Martin, a black Bentley, a red two-door Fiat and a pearl-white Range Rover. Dash walked toward the SUV, but changed his mind. He decided to take the convertible instead. He wanted to see Lark's hair blow in the wind. He put his treasures in the passenger seat of the Aston Martin and sped off down the driveway. He was sure Lark was awake by now and he wanted to return as quickly as he could, before she thought he had totally abandoned her. As he drove back to the hotel, a sense of joy filled his spirit. He had never felt this type of euphoria over a woman before—not even Heather. Though he hadn't known Lark for long, Dash had no doubt he had found the love of his life.

Chapter 11

Lark stretched her arms wide and, with her eyes still closed, she rubbed her hand on the opposite side of the bed. She expected to feel Dash's muscular body lying there, but the space he had occupied the night before was cold and empty. Lark opened her eyes and scanned the room. No Dash. She flipped back the covers and stepped out of bed. Her first thought was that he was in the shower. She padded across the room in her bare feet to the bathroom. She pushed back the door. No Dash.

"Where is he?" she wondered aloud.

Lark stood there for a moment and then turned around, went over to the nightstand, picked up the house phone and asked the operator to connect her to Dash Migilio's room. The line rang several times before the voice mail intercepted the call. Lark hung up without leaving a message and sat on the side of the bed. She wondered where he could have gone this early. They had shared such a special night together and Lark couldn't believe that he had left while she was still asleep. She had planned on ordering room service, having breakfast in bed and another round of mind-blowing sex before going back to the mill, but now Dash was gone. Her mind started playing the "What if" game.

What if he lied about not having a girlfriend?

What if he's like that jerk Edwin from the online dating site and is engaged to that girl in the picture?

What if he just wanted to sleep with me?

What if now that he's made his conquest, he doesn't want anything else to do with me?

The more Lark ran the different scenarios through her mind, the madder she became. She had allowed herself to get swept up in the moment, and now that the moment had passed, regret filled the space happiness had occupied only a few hours ago.

She stood and stormed back to the bathroom to clean her body of any evidence of their naughty evening. Under the spray of the shower, she lathered her body with shower gel and scrubbed her skin. Lark tried cleansing her mind as well and thought whatever was going on with Dash, she didn't care. She needed to forget about their one night of bliss. Lark had come to Italy to take care of business, and that was exactly what she was going to do, with or without the sexy young designer.

After showering, she ordered coffee from room service and then dressed in a khaki pantsuit—one of her original designs—a sheer flora blouse and a pair of coral-colored flats. She dusted her face with translucent powder, applied lipstick and combed her hair.

There was a knock at the door. Lark paused, thinking it might be Dash. She crossed the room, took a deep breath and opened the door.

"Good morning, miss. Here's your coffee," the room-service attendant said, holding a silver tray with a white carafe and two small containers.

"Hello. You can put it over there on the table."

"Can I get you anything else?"

"No, thank you."

Once the attendant left, Lark sat on the small sofa and poured a cup of coffee with cream and sugar. As she drank her coffee, she couldn't help but think of Dash. A part of her was disappointed that he hadn't shown up.

"Oh well," she said aloud.

She finished the coffee, grabbed her purse and a pair of oversize sunglasses off the nightstand and bolted out the door. She didn't have the driver's phone number, but she planned to hail a taxi downstairs.

"Hey, where's the fire?" Dash asked, standing in the doorway.

"I'm going to the mill," Lark said sternly, without making eye contact. She refused to let herself get caught up in his charm yet again. Last night she had been momentarily sidetracked, but now it was business as usual.

"We don't have to be there until later. I've planned…"

Lark cut him off. "I'd prefer to go now, approve the samples and get back to New York. I have a company to run."

Dash reached out to hug Lark, but she took a step back. "What's wrong?" he asked. "You seem distant."

Lark crossed her arms tightly against her chest. "Look, Dash, if you had to sneak out in the wee hours of the morning to check in with your girlfriend back in New

York, then so be it. Let's not kid ourselves and pretend this wasn't just a one-night stand," Lark spouted.

"For one, I told you before I don't have a girlfriend. Two, I didn't sneak out. I walked out quietly so as not to disturb you. And three, our evening of making love was far from a one-night stand." Dash pulled Lark to him and gave her a strong, manly kiss.

Lark tried to resist, but she melted like a cube of ice under warm running water once his lips touched hers. He had set her straight in no uncertain terms and she believed his every word.

"I left early to plan a surprise for you," he told her.

"A surprise? What type of surprise?"

Dash took her by the hand. "Come on. You'll see."

The lobby was filled with tourists and tour guides assembling to embark on an excursion to Florence and the surrounding area. As Lark and Dash moved through the crowd, toward the exit, she saw people with cameras hanging around their necks. Some were fiddling with maps and speaking in various languages about the day ahead.

"They seem excited," she commented.

"As they should be. This land is magnificent—filled with ancient wonder," Dash remarked with pride.

"I wish I could hop on the tour bus and join them. Whenever I'm in Italy, I'm always rushing, going from vendor to vendor and attending shows. I never have time to relax and truly enjoy myself."

"Your wish is my command."

"What do you mean?"

"We're going to take a break from business for at least a few hours and have an enjoyable picnic in the countryside."

Lark's face lit up. "Do we have time?"

"Of course. There's no need to rush. Have you forgotten that my family owns the mill? Marco will have the samples ready whenever we arrive. You're on my turf now and I'm calling the shots."

Lark found the authority in Dash's voice appealing. She was accustomed to leading the charge. Letting go of the reins—at least for a little while—felt liberating.

"Where's the driver?" she asked once they were outside.

"You're looking at him. I went by my parents' villa earlier and picked up my car," he said, leading her toward the convertible.

"Is this your car?"

"Yep."

"That's the Aston Martin BD5 from *Skyfall,* except in the James Bond movie, the car had a hard top," Lark said, admiring the spiffy sports car.

"I see you know your cars. I'm impressed. I had the car remolded to make it into a convertible."

"It's a beauty! I'm a huge fan of vintage cars. If I didn't live in Manhattan, I'd probably have at least two—a red '67 Mustang and an Aston Martin."

"You're a woman after my own heart. I love cars, too. Why don't you drive?" Dash said, handing her the key.

"Are you serious?"

"Of course." He moved around to the driver's door and opened it for her.

Lark put on her sunglasses, slid into the gently worn leather seat and ran her hands across the chrome steering wheel.

After putting the picnic basket and blanket in the trunk, Dash settled into the passenger seat. He told Lark how to exit the hotel and find the main road. They headed out of the city and soon were driving through the lush countryside. Rolling hills of emerald-green grass surrounded them, and the fresh citrus smell from lemon trees permeated the air as they whizzed along.

"You drive these roads as if you've done this before," Dash remarked.

"No, this is my first time. Your car drives like a dream. It handles the curves with such precision."

"Thanks. I have it serviced on a regular basis, even though I don't live here."

"I was so excited about getting behind the wheel that I didn't even ask where we're going."

"To Livorno. It's a quaint costal town and I know of the perfect spot to have a picnic. It's high above the city, where there are magnificent views of the sea."

"Sounds divine. How far?"

"A little over an hour."

"Oh, is that all? I could drive this car all day," Lark said, beaming.

The drive was pleasant, with the sun bright in a clear, azure-blue sky and the soft wind blowing through their hair. Their conversation was limited except for an occasional directive from Dash. Lark was absorbed in the moment, basking in the experience of driving her dream car. The kilometers ticked by until they were at their destination.

"Oh, wow! You were right. This is a gorgeous view," Lark said, stepping out of the car and looking out over the sapphire-blue sea.

Dash came up behind her, hugged her by the waist and kissed her neck. "It's postcard perfect." He released her, retrieved the basket from the trunk and spread the blanket on the grassy meadow.

Lark took off her shoes and jacket before kneeling down on the cashmere blanket, which had the colors of the Italian flag. "What's in the basket?"

"We have homemade olive tapenade, tomato-basil focaccia, cheese, prosciutto and melon," he said, taking out the items one by one. "And what Italian meal could be complete without vino?"

"Nice spread. Where did you get all of this?"

"I can't take the credit. Sophia put it together for me."

"Who's Sophia?" Lark asked.

"She's my housekeeper. Actually, she's more than just a housekeeper and cook. She's more like an aunt. She's been with our family since I was little and I adore her."

"Well, aren't you just the spoiled little rich boy?" Lark teased.

"I might be wealthy, but I'm far from spoiled. I plan to make a mark on the fashion world and not rest on my family's laurels."

Lark searched Dash's face, which had a stern expression, and she could see that he was serious. "I'm sorry if I offended you."

"No worries. Of course, I could easily kick back and spend my trust fund globe-trotting and entertaining random women along the way, but that type of hedonistic lifestyle isn't for me. One day my designs will be among the ranks of Valentino, Armani and Versace."

Hearing Dash speak so strongly about his future and living his life with integrity, instead of living off his family's money, endeared him to Lark all the more.

"I like your passion. I feel the same way about my

designs. Even though I'm the chief operating officer of RR, I want to one day earn a CFDA for my creativity."

Dash leaned over and kissed Lark on the lips. "I'm sure you will, sweetheart. You are really talented. We make a great team."

"Yes, we do."

They enjoyed the afternoon lounging on the blanket, eating and drinking wine. The more time she spent with Dash, the more smitten Lark was becoming. Though there was a gap in their ages, they were on the same plane both personally and professionally. Lark couldn't help but wonder if she had finally found her match. The thought was thrilling and frightening at the same time. Could she possibly have a future with a man born in a completely different decade?

Chapter 12

Lark's morning had begun with doubt and trepidation—she had thought that Dash had taken their night of bliss lightly. Dash had proved her wrong, not by using mere words, but by taking the time to orchestrate an impromptu picnic. The location he'd chosen, atop a hill overlooking turquoise waters, was tranquil and romantic. The food his housekeeper had prepared was light and tasteful. Lark subscribed to the philosophy that it wasn't what a person said, but what he did that spoke volumes. And Dash's actions that afternoon had shown her she was more than a casual-sex partner to him. She knew from experience that men who wanted only intercourse didn't bother to plan outings. Those men called in the middle of the night for what they wanted and fled shortly thereafter with no regard for the feelings of their sexual partner.

This was exactly the type of afternoon she needed

to ease the stress of running a major design firm. After her grandfather had passed away and her father retired, the business had been left to her. Lark's father had been reluctant to let his daughter take over the reins and had even offered to postpone his retirement. He had thought that she was too young to run the company. Lark had assured her father she was more than capable of not only running the business but of increasing sales exponentially. The fashion industry was tougher than she had imagined, and growing the business hadn't been an easy task.

"Thanks for such a lovely afternoon," she said as they packed up.

Dash finished folding the blanket and gave her a passionate kiss. "The pleasure was all mine. I enjoy being with you. Our conversations flow effortlessly."

"Yes, they do. It feels as if we've known each other for years."

"If we had more time, I'd take you on a tour of the village. It's really old and quaint, untouched by the modernization of time."

Lark looked down the hill, where she could see winding streets and people milling about in the distance. "I would have loved that. I like visiting small villages, checking out their wares and buying something unique. Maybe next time."

"So do I. You never know what you're going to find. We'll be sure to visit next time," Dash said, putting the containers back in the basket.

Thinking about how their business trip had morphed into a mini romantic holiday, Lark couldn't help but smile. This was the perfect diversion from her hectic life back in New York, where she worked nonstop trying to take the business to the next level. Her smile quickly faded when she thought about Darcy and what her friend would think of the unexpected turn of events. Lark was positive Darcy would disapprove.

"What's the pensive look for?" Dash asked.

"I was imagining what my friend Darcy would think of our, uh…love connection. She has strict rules about the dating game. She doesn't believe a woman should be the aggressor. She says men are hunters and they like the thrill of the chase."

"Yes, that's true to a certain extent. But your bold move last night on the dance floor was refreshing. You're a woman who knows what she wants and isn't afraid to go after it. That's why you're so successful."

"Thanks, but I'm sure Darcy won't see it that way. She also doesn't think workplace romances are healthy and usually end up badly."

"Your friend Darcy is quite opinionated, isn't she? Have you two been friends for long?"

"Even though she doesn't bite her tongue, she's my best friend. She was my mentor at RR when I first started. She took me under her wing, teaching me not only about business but about the ways of men."

"I see. Is she married?"

"No, she isn't."

"Well, maybe if she loosens some of her rules when it comes to the opposite sex, she would find a husband."

Lark weighed Dash's words. He was right. Darcy had become extremely cynical.

"I'm so glad you didn't take her advice. See what you would have missed out on if you had," Dash said, opening his arms wide to showcase his body.

Lark walked close, wrapped her arms around his

waist, leaned up and kissed him. "Like you said, I know what I want and go after it!"

They finished packing under the setting sun. As they drove along the countryside on the way to the mill, the sky morphed into a brilliant burnt orange with soft ribbons of gray clouds woven throughout, resembling an oil painting spectacular enough to rival the masters.

"The countryside here is so beautiful. You're lucky to have spent your summers here," Lark said. She looked over at Dash, who was now behind the wheel.

"Yes, I had a wonderful childhood. I just wish I'd had sisters and brothers to share it with."

"You're an only child, too? I always wanted a baby sister, but my mother swore she wasn't going through childbirth again. I guess it was too painful for her."

"My mom said the same thing, only in Italian," he said with a chuckle. "See, that's one more thing we have in common."

"If I ever have children, I'll have at least two."

Lark could imagine Dash fathering her children. She wanted to ask if he planned to have kids, but she thought against it. She didn't want to scare him off, so she changed the subject.

"Are you sure it's not too late to go to the mill?" Lark had expected to preview the samples earlier that afternoon. During their quaint picnic, she had lived in the moment, without giving work a second thought.

"Absolutely not. We'll be there shortly. Here in Florence, we don't live to work. We work to live. We eat well and enjoy what's really important out of life. Family, friends and laughter take precedence over eighty-hour work weeks and trying to make more money than the next guy."

"That's a healthy way of living. I need to subscribe to that philosophy."

"Maybe after the spring/summer shows are over we can take a few days off, return to Italy and not only explore Florence, but also spend a few days in Venice."

"Sounds heavenly. I've always wanted to take a gondola ride at midnight underneath the stars."

"Now, that's one date I wouldn't miss. We can even explore some of the shops that make those ornate Venetian masks."

"I can see myself in a black sequined mask."

"A friend of mine gives an annual masquerade ball. You could wear it there."

"I would love to. Dash, you've really made this trip special. Now I'm anxious to see the samples. I have a lot riding on this upcoming line. Now that RR has a new lead designer, I'm sure the critics will be circling to see if we can survive without Sebastian."

"You have no worries there. Your former designer may have had more years of experience, but I assure you, my designs coupled with your ideas will catapult RR ahead of the pack," Dash said.

"I hope you're right." Lark took a deep breath and wondered if she should confide in Dash. She had been carrying a heavy burden for months, and the pressure of keeping it to herself was becoming too much to bear. "Dash, I need to tell you something."

"What's wrong? You sound serious."

"The truth is, the sales numbers at Randolph on the Runway have been dwindling these past few seasons. I was hoping the orders from the last show would have pulled the company out of the red, but they didn't. I've exhausted the reserve fund I had set aside for emergencies, and if our new line isn't successful, I'm going to have to start laying people off, which I would really hate to do. I've already trimmed the budget as much as possible without affecting the staff. The thought of taking away someone's livelihood is heartbreaking."

Dash reached over and put his hand on her leg. "Don't worry, Lark. I promise you, it won't come to that. The new collection will be a success. I've got your back."

Lark breathed a sigh of relief. She had been apprehensive about revealing RR's financial predicament, but now that she had, she felt reassured. Although they hadn't broached the subject of being in a relationship, sharing her problems with Dash made Lark feel as if they were on the track to exclusivity.

When they arrived at the mill, Marco greeted them with open arms. *"Buonasera!"*

"Good evening, Marco. Sorry we're so late," Lark said as she entered the building.

"No problema. The samples are ready." Marco walked them over to a drafting table and revealed the strike-offs of Lark's designs.

Lark picked up a piece of fabric and inspected it thoroughly. She had an eye for detail, so she looked for inconsistencies in the color and pattern. The hues were correct and the pattern was exactly as she had designed it. Lark had experienced major flaws in the past with some vendors, but she didn't have any complaints this time. She rubbed the silk between her thumb and index finger, feeling for the desired softness. Lark took her time studying the samples.

"Well…what do you think?" Dash asked, standing over her shoulder.

"The way a dress moves is determined by the quality of the material, and this silk is exquisite! Well done. Bravo!" Lark thanked Marco with a warm hug.

"You approve?" Marco asked.

"Yes! When can you start production?"

"Randolph. We will begin manufacturing first thing in the morning."

"That's great news!"

By the time they departed the mill, Lark had a renewed sense of hope. With Dash by her side, she knew without a doubt that RR would rule the runway and become profitable once again.

Chapter 13

There was complete pandemonium at Randolph on the Runway when Lark and Dash returned from Italy. Their trip had been cut short when Lark had received an urgent call from her assistant to inform her of the impending disaster. Lark had wanted to spend more time in Italy with Dash. They were getting closer with each passing day and she hadn't wanted to break their momentum. But duty called. Lark immediately told Angelica to book them on the next flight back to New York.

Lark and Dash had gone straight to the office from the airport. She was jet-lagged, but sleep was a luxury that she couldn't afford. Her romantic romp in Italy was over and now it was back to strictly business between them. Lark was seated at the oval table in the conference room, surrounded by the division heads. They were meeting to discuss what had transpired while Lark and Dash were in Florence.

"Explain to me how our computer system could have been breached," Lark said, directing her comment to Edward, the head of the IT department.

"Somehow, a Trojan virus invaded the company's main hard drive and wiped out the CAD program," Edward said nervously.

"Edward, you've already explained that part! My question is, how can a virus delete all of our design files? Don't we have firewalls and online security systems in place to prevent this type of situation from happening?"

Lark was steaming mad, but she was trying to maintain her composure and not unleash her fury on just one person.

"Of course we do, but the virus eluded the firewalls," Edward responded.

"Could this have happened from one of our employees opening a corrupt email?" Dash, who was sitting across the table from Lark, asked.

"Yes, that's a possibility. An email could have had an encrypted attachment."

"Edward, why isn't your team on top of this? This is the last thing I need to deal with!" Lark shook her head in frustration.

"Trust me, we are. But new viruses invade the internet on a daily basis."

Lark exhaled hard. "Look, we can go around and around about why and how our system was compromised—the bottom line now is, how do we get past this? Can the files be retrieved?"

"I'm afraid not," Edward responded.

"Are you serious?" she yelled, no longer able to control her temper.

"What about the backup files?" Dash asked, thumping the tip of his pencil on the table.

"Uh…those were erased, too," Edward responded hesitantly.

"So you're telling me the designers have to input their drawings into the CAD system once more?" Lark asked.

Luckily, Lark had a company policy of sketching out designs on a drawing pad, an antiquated method she had adopted from her grandfather. Initially, she had fought her grandfather on what she had thought to be a waste of time. Now she was relieved she had listened. Otherwise the entire new line would have been history. Lark couldn't believe the misfortunes RR had been plagued with lately. First Sebastian going off the rails and now an untimely computer breach.

"Yes, all of the drawings will have to be reentered," Edward replied.

Lark turned to Aisha, a senior designer seated to her right. "Aisha, how long do you think it'll take for your team to reproduce their designs?"

"Maybe a week or two," the petite woman answered.

Lark slumped in her chair as if someone had sucker punched her. "We don't have two weeks. In order to get the new collection into production, the drawings need to be in the system by the end of the week."

"We'll just have to work around the clock to make that happen," Dash said.

"Not a problem," Aisha replied.

Leaning on the edge of her chair, Lark put her elbows on the table and her head in her hands. She was silent for a few moments. "If the designs can be reentered by then, we'll have enough time to get them to the patternmakers before the deadline." She stood and arched her back. "Okay, people, rally your teams. Let's get the ball rolling. Time is a-ticking!"

Everyone began gathering their belongings and filing out of the room until Dash and Lark were the only two to remain. He rose from his seat and closed the door.

"Are you okay?"

"Not really. I can't let the company my grandfather founded go under. I assured my father that I was more than capable of running RR and increasing revenue. Now I'm not so sure." A tear was forming in Lark's eye, and she dropped her head.

Dash stood behind her and began massaging her shoulders. "It's going to be all right," he whispered in her ear.

"How can you be so sure? In this industry you're only as good as your last collection. It's easy to fall by the wayside."

"Trust me, that's not going to happen to RR. I looked around the conference table during the meeting and saw the dedication in the faces of everyone here. We all want the same thing, and that's for RR to succeed. If we have to work nonstop in order to get back on track, that's exactly what we're going to do. And I for one have a vested interest..."

Lark peered over her shoulder at Dash. "What's that?"

He turned her around so she was facing him and softly kissed her lips.

Lark took a step away from Dash and peered over at the plate-glass window to see if anyone was looking into the conference room. "We're not in Italy anymore.

We should cool it while we're in the office. I don't want the other employees to know that we're…involved. It doesn't look professional."

"I understand, but frankly, I don't care who knows. Although we haven't known each other for long, our connection is real and I truly care about you, Lark. Our time together in Florence wasn't some type of fleeting fling. I've never felt this way about a woman before."

She could see the sincerity in his eyes. "What way is that?" she asked.

"I could fall in love with you."

Lark's heart almost skipped a beat. In the middle of a near catastrophe, she had found her bedrock. Dash had come to her rescue once again. He was proving to be the real deal. "I feel the same way, but let's agree to keep our affair out of the office."

"Okay, on one condition," Dash said with a flirty expression.

"And what's that?"

"Once we're alone in private, you'll let me show you how much I care."

"You got yourself a deal," Lark replied, and then she gathered her belongings and strutted out of the conference room. Lark walked with a renewed sense of purpose on the way back to her office. She had found a solution to the computer crisis and knew that whatever mishap was tossed her way, she could handle it as long as Dash was by her side.

Chapter 14

After their dinner at a local Indian restaurant, Dash had taken Lark to his penthouse in the swanky Time Warner building. His apartment had vistas of both Columbus Circle and Central Park, and it was the perfect place to unwind. It had been a few days since the security breach in RR's computer system and the entire design staff had rolled up their sleeves and gone the extra mile, working until the wee hours of the morning to ensure all of the designs were reinserted into the CAD program by the deadline.

Lark and Dash had been inundated with work and hadn't made love since they'd returned from Italy. He was eager to lose himself again in her loving.

"Would you like a glass of port?" Dash asked.

"Sure," Lark said as she stood at the window, admiring the view below.

Dash poured them a glass of the after-dinner elixir, turned on a jazz CD and walked over to Lark. "Here you go." He handed her a glass and then clicked his glass against hers. "To finally having an evening together outside of work."

"I'll drink to that." Lark took a sip of the ruby-colored liquor. "Hopefully we won't have to deal with any more mishaps until after the collection is produced, the shows are over and the orders are filled."

"I'm not worried about whatever comes our way. We make an awesome team and together can handle anything."

"I agree."

"Enough work talk. I haven't had you alone in days and I've been dying to kiss those luscious lips of yours."

Dash took Lark's glass and placed it on a nearby table, along with his. He then caressed her waist, bringing her closer, and touched his lips to hers, giving her a series of soft kisses. The tender smooches intensified until their tongues were dancing a heated duet. Dash could feel his member swelling. He pressed firmly against Lark's pelvis so that she could feel his want for her. He stopped, took her by the hand and said, "Let's go in the bedroom."

Dash led Lark through the large living room, down a hallway filled with artwork and into his master bedroom.

"Take off your clothes," he said, unbuckling his belt.

Dash watched as Lark reached underneath her skirt and removed her panties.

"How's that for starters?" she asked, tossing the lace underwear toward him.

"Perfect. Keep going." Dash unbuttoned his pants

and let them drop to the floor. He rubbed the front of his boxer briefs, showcasing the outline of his firm manhood. "See the effect you have on me?"

"Hmm, nice!" Lark took off her blouse, unhooked her bra and shook her breasts. "You like?"

"I do indeed." Dash reached out and rubbed her nipples. "Now, take off your skirt."

Lark unzipped her skirt and stepped out of it.

"Looking at your body is making me so hard," he said.

Dash took Lark's hand, led her to the bed, opened the nightstand and took out a pack of condoms. He suited up and wedged himself between Lark's legs, pressed her thighs apart and began rotating his hips, grinding deeper into her before pumping feverishly. She wrapped her arms around his neck and thrust her hips forward, matching his rhythm.

He was hungry for Lark and was having a hard time controlling himself. Her warm, wet canal hugged his penis tightly and the sensation was causing his army of men to march to a climax. The more he tried to hold back, the harder it became. Dash held on to the headboard as his back arched and beads of sweat sprouted onto his forehead. He exploded into the condom and then collapsed onto the bed next to Lark.

After catching his breath, he said, "I'm so sorry about that."

"About what?" Lark asked, lying back on the pillows.

"For not giving you a chance to come first. Just so you know, I'm not a selfish lover. I'm a pleaser."

"I already know that. You more than pleased me back in Florence." Lark eased to the side of the bed and climbed out.

"Hey, where are you going?" Dash said, gently tugging her by the arm.

"I should get back to work," she said.

Dash glanced over to the nightstand at his sleek timepiece, which looked more like a flute than a clock. "It's late. You might as well stay the night."

"What about work?"

"Nearly all of the designs are in the system. The fabric will be shipped by the end of the week. So we're on schedule." Dash rubbed her naked behind. "Besides, I haven't gotten enough of you."

"We just made love."

"I wouldn't call that *making love*—that was a quickie. Now we need to really relax and enjoy ourselves. We've been working nonstop. A few hours away from the office won't hurt," he said, gently pulling her closer and closer toward him, until she was back in bed.

"One second," Dash added, hopping to his feet.

After a few minutes, he returned with an ice bucket filled with champagne, two flutes and a red-and-black box tucked under his arm.

"What's that?" Lark asked.

"A board game," he said, putting the box on the bed.

"A game? I thought we were gearing up for round two."

"Oh, we are. This isn't just any game. It's a provocative board game for adults only," he said, pouring them each a glass of champagne and handing her a flute.

Lark took a sip. "Do tell."

"My friends Warren and LaDonna created this game called Secret VII. It's designed to intensify foreplay." Dash opened the lid, took out the game pieces, which included colored cards, a pair of dice and an audible timepiece, and assembled them on the bed. "There are four different colored cards—blue, yellow, red and black— ranging from mild to wild. The colors signify the intensity of the sexual acts to perform. The blue cards are mild, with suggestive words like 'Blow in my ear.' The yellow cards are for medium heat. The red cards are for wild intensity, and the black cards are blank, designed for you to create your own sexual fantasy."

"Oh, I like this game already."

"I thought you would. Now we each pick seven cards and then roll the dice. The person to roll a seven picks first," Dash explained.

Lark put her glass on the nightstand, took the dice in her hands, blew on them and shook them onto the bed. "Oh, shoot!" she exclaimed, looking down at the eight she'd rolled.

"My turn." Dash rolled snake eyes.

They continued rolling the dice until Lark got the lucky number. "Bingo! A seven! Now what?"

"I have to choose a card from your hand and do whatever it says for two minutes." Dash picked one of her pleasure cards.

"I see you're starting off mild," she said, referring to the blue card he had selected.

"Yep. I don't want to turn you out on the first round," he teased.

"So, what does the card say?" Lark asked anxiously.

Dash read the card. "For me to stare at your naked body with my most sensuous look."

Lark didn't hesitate. She leaned on the headboard, bent her knees and cocked her legs. "Can you see?"

"Oh, yeah." Dash set the audible timer and moved closer to get a better look, leaned on his elbow and smiled slyly. He gave her his best come-hither look, staring intently at her nakedness.

"Am I making you hot?" Lark asked.

"You most certainly are," Dash answered, without breaking his concentration.

After the timer sounded, they resumed rolling the dice until Dash rolled a seven and it was Lark's turn to pull a card from his hand.

"I'm skipping yellow and going straight to red," Lark said.

"Okay, Ms. Caliente, what's the next task?"

"It's one of my favorite numbers—sixty-nine!"

"And one of my favorite positions," Dash remarked.

They each put their cards on the nightstand and quickly assumed the position. The intensity of their mouths' movements increased, bringing them both to the brink of orgasm. Neither could talk, but their moans were speaking volumes.

He stiffened his tongue and stuck it as far as he could into her moistness. Dash could taste Lark's juices as they oozed into his mouth. He withdrew his penis from her mouth and ejaculated onto the sheet.

"I love Secret VII! That was awesome!" Lark said, panting. She turned her body around and rested her head on his hairy chest.

"Yes, it was!"

Dash closed his eyes. Instead of falling asleep, he envisioned a life with Lark. She was everything he wanted in a woman—sexy, smart and compassionate. In his mind's eye, he saw them traveling around the world, finding inspiration for their designs and making love on different continents. Dash had always been attracted to older women. He admired their style and maturity.

Until now, he had never dated one. Dash opened his eyes, gazed over at Lark and knew that she would be his now and forever.

Chapter 15

Lark and Darcy were having lunch at a hip French bistro in SoHo. The restaurant was bustling with businesspeople, models, ad execs dining on expense accounts and Ladies Who Lunch. Lark and Darcy were ensconced in a cozy corner booth away from the fray, compliments of the manager, a friend of Darcy's. Spread before them was a seafood tier of mussels, clams on the half shell, escargots and oysters.

"How was Florence? I called your office when you were out and your assistant told me you were in Italy for business," Darcy said, sipping a champagne cocktail.

Lark's face lit up at the mere mention of her Italian adventure. "It was *molto bene!*" she answered, gesturing her hands in the air.

"Oh, so you're Italian now?" Darcy joked.

"I'm bilingual." She giggled. "I picked up a few words here and there while I was in Italy."

Darcy eyed her friend curiously. "Did you learn the language from your new lead designer? Didn't you say he's Italian-American?"

"Yes, I did. He taught me a lot," Lark answered cryptically.

"Really?" Darcy leaned forward. "What else did he teach you?"

Lark exhaled, deciding whether or not to divulge her romantic rendezvous to Darcy. During their last outing, she and Darcy had discussed how detrimental workplace liaisons could be. Lark was nearly bursting at the seams. She wanted to shout to the world that she had found the perfect man, but she hadn't told a soul. Lark quickly weighed her options and decided that if Darcy was her friend, she wouldn't be judgmental.

"Well, if you must know, I crossed the line with Dash. We're not simply coworkers any longer." Lark sipped her iced tea and waited for Darcy's reaction.

"Why would you do that? Didn't you say he's in a relationship?"

"Initially, I thought he was. The woman in the picture was his ex. He assured me their relationship is long over with."

"Are you sure? You know how some men can lie at the drop of a dime to get you into bed."

"Dash isn't like that. He's honest and doesn't play games," Lark said, immediately coming to his defense.

Darcy shook her head as if in disapproval. "Even if that is the case, do you think it's a wise idea to get involved with one of your employees? You have enough on your plate with the upcoming spring/summer show. If it doesn't work out, you'll have to see each other on a regular basis, and since you work so closely together, that could be quite uncomfortable. Trust me, I know from experience."

"I understand the odds are against workplace romances, but this is different. For once, I went with my heart instead of my head. The moment felt right, so I said…'Why not?' Darcy, I know your philosophy of hanging back and letting the man do the pursuing. In the past that's worked out well, but the years are swiftly rolling by and I can't afford to sit on the sidelines anymore and wait for a man to pick me. I don't want to be a spinster with nothing but work to occupy my time."

"You mean like me?"

Lark hadn't wanted to hurt her friend's feelings, but that was exactly what she had been thinking. "Well, you can still get married if you want to, but…"

"…it's too late for me to have children. I've never told anyone this before, but that's my biggest regret in life. I was laser focused on my career during my childbearing years, thinking I had all the time in the world to get married and have babies. If I knew then what I know now, I would have taken the time to cultivate a meaningful relationship. I let so many good men slip through my fingers over the years. Men who would have made good fathers. Do you think your guy would be a good dad?" Darcy asked.

"Yes, I do. We haven't broached the subject of marriage and kids, but I can see he's a kind and caring man. He would make the perfect husband and father."

The second Lark spoke those words, she wanted them to materialize into reality. There was no denying she was falling for Dash and falling hard. In the past, she would have pumped the brakes and slowed things down, but time was no longer on her side. If she wanted to have a child—which she did—she needed to be proactive. Lark loved Darcy dearly, but she didn't want to end up alone, with no one to snuggle up to at night.

"Lark, I hope you're right and this isn't just a work fling. I can hear it in your voice that you truly care for this man."

"I really do. Darcy, what we have is the real deal. I can feel it in my heart."

"I'm happy for you, Lark. Let's all go out for drinks soon so I can meet him. Once I see the two of you together, I'll know if he's genuine or not."

"Darcy, you sound like an overprotective big sister."

"We may not be related, but I consider us family, and I look out for my people."

"Point taken."

As they were talking, Lark's cell phone rang. "Hello?… WHAT!…You've got to be kidding…Okay, I'm on my way."

"What's wrong?" Darcy asked once Lark had disconnected the call.

"That was my assistant. The fabric I ordered in Florence is stuck at customs!"

"Why? You get shipments from Italy all the time."

"I don't know what the problem is. I'm sorry, but I'm going to have to cut our lunch short and head back to the office." Lark quickly grabbed her tote and kissed Darcy on the cheek.

"No worries. I totally understand. Let me know if I can do anything."

"I will. Talk to you later."

Lark rushed out of the door, walked to the corner of Broadway and hailed a taxi. On the way back to work, she called Dash. His cell phone rang and rang before going to voice mail.

"Where are you? We have an urgent problem. Call me as soon as you get this."

She then called the office and asked her assistant to put her through to Dash's office. Again his line rang without an answer. Lark disconnected the call without leaving a message. She gazed out the window, wondering where Dash could be. It wasn't like him not to answer her call.

"Can you speed it up?" she asked the taxi driver, anxious to get back to the office as soon as possible.

"No problem."

The driver stepped on the gas and began weaving in and out of traffic, nearly having an accident or two along the way. Within minutes, he was pulling in front of Randolph on the Runway. Lark tossed him a twenty for his valiant effort and hurried inside.

Upstairs, she walked swiftly through the floor, passed her office and made a beeline to Dash's. She needed to speak with him as soon as possible to find out if he knew about the delay in customs. The company had never had a problem receiving goods from Europe, and for the life of her, she couldn't understand what the issue might be.

Maybe Marco's people didn't fill out the paperwork properly, or maybe customs has our shipment mixed up with another company, she thought.

Lark was ready to bombard Dash with a litany of questions, but she was stopped in her tracks by the sight before her.

She stood there and watched through the glass wall of Dash's office as the blonde from the picture on Dash's tablet planted a juicy kiss on his lips. From what Lark could see, Dash wasn't resisting the beautiful woman's advances. The blonde had her body pressed against Dash's and her arms draped around his neck. Lark couldn't believe her eyes. She was frozen in shock for a moment. Before Dash could catch her staring, she quickly composed herself, swiveled around on her heels and headed to her office. She was walking so fast that she nearly tripped over her feet.

Lark brushed past Angelica, who was trying to speak with her about the customs issue.

"Ms. Randolph, I'm so glad you're back. What are we going to do about customs? I've been trying to get them to release the shipment, but I haven't had any luck. You're going to have to call the supervisor and speak with him."

"I'm sorry, Angelica. I can't talk about that at the moment. I'll have to get back to you." Lark couldn't think straight. She needed to collect her thoughts, so she went into her office and shut the door.

For the first time since the renovation of the office, Lark wished for a solid wall between herself and the rest of the office. She was on the verge of tears and didn't want her waterworks to be on display.

Lark walked over to the window and stared down at the people milling about. She instantly thought back to Darcy's earlier comment: *...some men can lie at the drop of a dime to get you into bed.*

Lark had emphatically defended Dash, but judging by what she had just witnessed, he and the blonde were still very much involved. Why else would he let her kiss him in his office for everyone to see?

With her back to the door, Lark allowed the tears she had been trying to suppress to fall. She had totally misjudged Dash, and now she regretted letting herself get involved with him. Obviously he wasn't as mature as she had thought. He was a young man, still sowing his oats.

Chapter 16

Dash peeled Heather's arms from around his neck and stepped back. He was appalled. "What do you think you're doing?" he asked with an angry expression on his face.

"Giving you a congratulatory kiss. Randolph on the Runway is lucky to have such a brilliant designer," she said, gazing lovingly into his eyes.

"How did you know about my new position?" Dash asked, brushing off her flirtatious advance. His feelings for Heather had long faded.

"There was a mention in the trades about you replacing Sebastian. What a deal for you. I know you always wanted your designs to be part of a major collection."

During college, before they had started dating, Heather and Dash had been friends and had shared their dreams of one day designing for a world-renowned fashion house.

"Thanks. I am excited about debuting my designs in the spring/summer shows."

"The article was nice, except there wasn't a picture of you, so I couldn't see your fabulous smile, which I miss. I decided to come here in person and congratulate you in the flesh. You're as handsome as ever."

Dash took in his former girlfriend. Her formerly long blond hair was now extremely short, and her slinky emerald-green jersey dress hugged her curves to perfection. She was still a knockout and most men would fall all over themselves trying to date her. But he no longer desired Heather. That ship had long ago sailed *and* sunk.

"Thanks, but a text message would have sufficed."

"Sometimes texting can be so impersonal. Remember back in college how we used to stay up late at night designing clothes? Our collaborations were so on point. We had sketch pads full of collections for men and women and could have gone into business together right after graduation."

"Of course I remember. I still have my old sketchbooks." Dash couldn't deny that he and Heather were a good design team.

"Does RR have any other designer positions open? I'd love to work alongside you again."

"Afraid not. All the positions are filled."

"Oh, that's too bad." Heather paused for a moment and then rubbed her hair. "You haven't said anything about my new haircut. Thought I'd try something different. I think it's sassy and sexy. Do you like it?"

"It's nice. Heather, I don't have time for small talk. I'm in the middle of work. I'm going to have to cut this visit short."

"Dash, I miss you… I miss us," she blurted out.

"Where is this coming from? I haven't seen or heard

from you in over a year. What we had ended long ago and I've moved on. And even if I hadn't, I told you before that I'm not into that poly-whatever thing. I don't share my partner or my body."

"Polyamory. Anyway, I'm not a polyamorist anymore. Stacy and I broke up. I moved out months ago and have my own place in the West Village, which is big enough for two people. Dash, I made a huge mistake and I'm sorry. Being apart from you has made me realize how important you are to me. Let's start over. Move in with me. This time, it'll just be the two of us, I promise. Dash, I'll never forget when you took me to Italy. It was my first time overseas and you treated me like a princess, showing me all over Florence and introducing me to your family. We could have traveled throughout Europe like you had planned if I hadn't spoiled everything. Can you ever forgive me?" she asked, nearly in tears.

"I don't have any hard feelings, Heather. The past is the past."

She stepped closer and tried to plant another kiss on Dash, but he moved to the other side of the desk, out of her grasp.

"Heather, getting back together isn't going to happen. I'm in a relationship now."

"Oh," she said with disappointment in her voice. "She's a lucky woman. I hope you're happy."

"No, I'm the lucky one, and yes, I'm extremely happy. I don't mean to be rude, but I really have to get back to work. Take care of yourself, Heather."

Dash led her to the door and watched his past walk out of his life for good. He felt no remorse. What had previously been a hurtful experience was now nothing more than a distant memory. Although he and Lark hadn't discussed exclusivity, he knew without a doubt they had a future together.

He left his office and made his way to Lark's. She had been out to lunch when he received an urgent call from U.S. Customs. Dash had Lark's assistant call to alert her to the situation, while he made a few calls in an effort to pinpoint the problem. Heather had momentarily diverted his attention with her regrets. Now he was back on track and needed to tell Lark what he had learned.

When Dash reached Lark's office, the door was closed, but he could see through the plate-glass window that she was sitting behind her desk and on the phone.

"Hi, Angelica, how's it going?" he said, standing in front of the assistant's desk.

Angelica was rapidly typing on her laptop. "Busy. What can I help you with, Dash?"

"I need to talk to Ms. Randolph," he said, taking a step toward Lark's door.

"Wait—don't go in there. She doesn't want to be disturbed."

"It's okay, Angelica. I'm sure Ms. Randolph won't mind." Dash knocked on Lark's door, but he went inside without waiting for an answer. He closed the door behind him so they could have a little privacy, took a seat across from her desk and waited for Lark to finish her telephone call.

"Thanks for your help, Marco. Yes, I'll let you know once the shipment arrives here at the office. Ciao."

"Listening to you speak Italian is turning me on." Dash reached across the desk and tried to touch Lark's hand, but she pulled it away.

"What do you want, Dash?"

"I talked to the head of customs and…"

"No need to explain. I called Marco and went over the declaration documents with him. We discovered the mistake."

"Yeah. The values on the forms were incorrect. I spoke with him, too."

"I'm surprised you had the time to speak with customs."

"Of course I have time, babe. The second I learned of the delay with customs I was on the phone with them, trying to straighten everything out. We can't have the fabric sitting in a warehouse for weeks. It'll throw off the production schedule."

"Yes, I know all of that, and don't call me *babe*. Dash, I think we need to cool it for a while. This is the second mishap in less than a week and I need to keep my focus on work and not on my personal life. There's a lot riding on this new collection."

Dash didn't respond. He felt as if the oxygen were being sucked out of his body. Twenty-four hours ago, they had shared an erotic evening, bonding and getting closer. Suddenly she was talking to him without any emotion, as if he were a stranger. "Lark, what's going on? Is everything okay?"

"I'm fine. What's going on with you?"

"What do you mean? I've been here at the office all day trying to put out this fire." Dash was totally perplexed. "Our relationship has nothing to do with the issues we're having at RR, and taking a step back isn't the answer. We're both professionals, and we can handle our work lives as well as our private ones. We've already proved that. I don't understand why you're suddenly having a change of heart."

"Look, I really don't have time for this discussion.

I'm running late for a meeting," she said with a tight voice as she picked her tablet off the desk.

Dash studied her face. Her lips were pursed and a frown line creased her brow. "Lark, what's really going on? I can see you're upset. Please talk to me. Whatever is going on, we can work it out."

"I don't know how you have time for business when you're busy entertaining guests on company time," Lark said and bolted out of the door.

Dash sat there in the wake of her cryptic message, dumbfounded. Lark fled so fast he didn't get a chance to ask what she meant. He leaned back in his chair, trying to decipher what she had meant. Dash held his chin with his thumb and index finger, pondering the situation.

"Oh, damn! Lark must have seen Heather kissing me through the glass!" Dash slapped the arm of the chair with the palm of his hand.

Heather had come back into his life at the most inopportune time. He could only imagine what had been going through Lark's mind when she witnessed his ex-girlfriend kissing him. Dash had to clarify the mix-up before Lark slipped away. He had walked into Lark's office certain they had a future together. But at this point he wasn't so sure.

Chapter 17

Lark drifted through the rest of the afternoon in a dense fog. Not only was her work life challenging, but her personal life was suddenly in a tailspin through no fault of her own. To prevent herself from crying in front of Dash, she had bolted out of her office, leaving him sitting there looking clueless. Even after Lark had dropped a hint about seeing him with his ex-girlfriend, Dash had seemed unfazed, as if he hadn't known what she was talking about. Lark wasn't sure if his innocence was an act or if he honestly didn't know what she had been referring to. In either case, she needed to put some space between herself and Dash in order to think straight.

Once her meetings for the day were over, Lark left the office. On her way to the elevator, Lark could see Dash was on the phone in his office. *He's probably talking to his girlfriend.*

"Whatever," she mumbled before boarding the elevator.

Outside, Lark kept pace with the bustling crowd of pedestrians along Seventh Avenue. There were tourists taking pictures of the sights in Times Square and posing with life-size cartoon characters, as well as businesspeople carrying briefcases on their way to places unknown. Lark didn't feel much like going home. She was fearful that a night at home alone would turn into a Pity Party, and she was determined not to shed any tears over Dash. If he wanted to rekindle the flames with his ex, that was his choice. They were not exclusive and he was free to do whatever he pleased. Lark had known that getting involved with the young designer could possibly have heartbreaking consequences, but she hadn't been prepared for it to happen so soon. Darcy had been right; Lark should never have gotten involved with Dash in the first place. Number one, he was too young for her, and number two, he was her employee. She should have known better, but now it was too late. The best thing she could do at this point was to move forward and forget about her lapse in judgment.

She shrugged off the feeling of doom as she walked inside a popular seafood restaurant. Lark bypassed the hostess stand and went directly to the bar.

"Good evening. What can I get for you?" the bartender asked.

"I'll have a double Manhattan."

"Coming right up."

As Lark waited for her cocktail, she heard her cell phone vibrate. She looked at the caller ID and saw that it was Dash. She swiped the face of the phone, sending his call directly to voice mail. She wasn't ready to speak with him just yet. Lark needed to get her emotions in check. She didn't want Dash to hear the jealously in her voice. She turned off the phone and tossed it back into her bag.

"Would you care to run a tab?" the bartender asked, putting a martini glass filled to the brim with garnet-colored liquid in front of her.

"Yes, I would," Lark said, reaching into her purse for her wallet.

"You can put her drink on my tab," a male voice said from behind her.

Lark turned slightly to see who was speaking. She took one look and nearly fell off the bar stool.

"Hello, Lark. How have you been?"

She stared at him before answering. He was as good-looking as ever. He wore a tailored navy blue pin-striped suit that fit his broad shoulders perfectly, a crisp white French-cuffed shirt and a muted pink tie. His chiseled face was clean-shaven and his mingled gray hair was cut to perfection. Lark could feel a knot forming in her throat as his piercing ebony eyes stared deeply into hers. She wasn't about to get caught up in his charms *again*. She slowly swiveled back around to the bar and took a sip of her Manhattan.

"I'm well, Edwin," she said as coolly as she could.

Edwin Spears was the guy she had met online who had wooed her with flowers and false promises of a happily ever after. Only he had already promised that fairy tale to someone else.

There was an empty bar stool next to her, and he took a seat without asking permission. "You're looking beautiful as ever."

Lark watched his eyes roam over her and she felt uncomfortable under his gaze. "Don't start, Edwin. I'm not in the mood for any more of your lies."

"Lark, please let me apologize for…"

"For what? For not telling me you were engaged?" she interrupted.

"Bartender, I'll have a dirty martini with three olives," he said, as if buying time before answering. He returned his attention to Lark. "Yes. I should have told you I was previously engaged, but we were just getting to know each other and I didn't want to ruin the present by talking about a past relationship."

"The woman who answered your phone seemed to be under the impression the two of you were on the way down the aisle."

"We were, and then we broke up. That's when I met you. Pamela and I have a history of breaking up and getting back together, but the last time she walked out on me, I swore it was over. I was tired of her drama. A friend of mine suggested that I join one of those dating sites. At first I was reluctant, but eventually uploaded my profile. You were the only woman who piqued my interest."

"Lucky me," Lark said drily.

"Lark, I honestly wanted to have a relationship with you. You're beautiful, smart and easy to talk to."

"If I was so easy to talk to, why weren't you honest with me? You could have saved me from having that unpleasant exchange with your fiancée. Edwin, I don't step on other women's toes by dating men who are taken. That's a strict rule of mine. I wouldn't have even accepted flowers from you."

Edwin put his hand on top of Lark's and rubbed her skin. "I'm so sorry. Can you please forgive me?"

Lark glanced down at his left hand, which was resting on hers, and quickly snatched her hand away. "Judging by that platinum-and-diamond band on your ring finger, looks like you married the drama."

Edwin looked sheepish as he moved his hand. "I didn't have much of a choice."

"I'm sure she didn't have a gun to your head."

"No, but you could say that it was a shotgun wedding. She's pregnant."

"Well, isn't that the oldest trap in the book?"

"We're married in name only. I'm not in love with her. Once the baby is born I plan to get a divorce. I only married Pamela because I want the child to have my last name."

"Oh, isn't that admirable of you," Lark said drily.

"Are you seeing anyone?"

Lark's mind flashed back to Dash. She had thought they were headed toward a meaningful relationship but she was wrong. "No, I'm not."

"Good."

"Excuse me?"

"Running into each other is fate. You're not in a relationship and I'm about to get divorced. Lark, there was chemistry between us and I think we deserve a second chance at happiness. Can we go upstairs and talk? I have a room where we can be alone."

"You've got to be kidding. I may be single but I'm not desperate." Lark scooted her stool back and stood. "Have a good life, Edwin." She didn't bother finishing her drink. Lark wasn't going to waste another second conversing with a married, womanizing liar.

Outside, Lark hailed a taxi. The cab drove up, and she got inside and told the driver her address. As they rode through Midtown traffic, she couldn't help but think back on the scene she'd witnessed in Dash's office. It didn't make sense to her that Dash would kiss his ex-girlfriend inside of his glass-encased office for everyone to see. They had gotten off to a solid start. She was even beginning to have genuine feelings for him. Dash didn't seem to be the lying, deceitful type, unlike Edwin. Had she totally misjudged Dash's intentions? Lark needed some answers. Work was intense enough, and she didn't need to be at odds with her senior designer.

Lark took her phone out of her purse and turned it on. She hit Redial and the line began ringing.

"We need to talk," she said the second Dash picked up.

"I know. I've been trying to call you, but your phone went straight to voice mail. Are you okay?"

"Not really. Can you come over to my place this evening? I don't want to talk about this over the phone."

"Of course. I'll be right over."

Lark gave Dash her address and disconnected the call. Her stomach began to tighten. What if her moral compass was off and she had put her trust in the wrong man yet again? Lark was beginning to think she would never find the perfect man to settle down with.

Chapter 18

Dash was relieved Lark had returned his call and invited him over. He detected by her cold tone that she was still upset. He could only imagine what must have been going through Lark's mind when she spotted Heather in his office with her arms draped around his neck, passionately kissing him. It had been only a few hours since Lark had rushed out of her office without giving him a chance to explain, but to Dash it felt like an eternity. He couldn't wait to talk to Lark so he could clear up the misunderstanding and get back on track with her. There was no way he was going to lose Lark over Heather's rash act.

He gathered an important document off his desk and slipped it into his messenger bag. While Lark was out of the office, he'd stayed late and cleared up the customs issue. Dash was not only dedicated to the company—he was also loyal to Lark, and tonight he planned to show her just how loyal and dedicated he was.

"Hey, Dash, are you headed out?" Jessica asked, rounding the corner of her cubicle the moment he stepped out of his office.

"I am. Why are you here so late? Did you have any problems with the CAD system?" he asked.

Dash noticed that the voluptuous junior designer had ditched her baggy clothes and had been coming to work dressing sexy. Today she wore an electric-blue, micro-miniskirt that barely covered her thick thighs and a sheer cobalt blouse that exposed her black lace bra.

"No, all of my designs are back in the system. You want to grab a drink? I really could use one after such a stressful day," she said, giving him a dreamy look.

This chick just won't give up, Dash thought. "No, thanks." He started to walk away, but then he turned back. "Oh…and, Jessica, just so you know, I'm seeing someone and I won't be having a drink with you tonight or any other night."

Jessica moved closer to Dash, nearly touching her double Ds to his chest. "That's okay. I don't mind sharing."

"Not going to happen. And when you come to work tomorrow, kindly clean your belongings out of the cubicle…"

"You're firing me?" she asked in shock.

"No, but I'm putting you on notice here and now. If you don't start acting and dressing professionally, you're out of here. Jessica, you're a talented designer, and with the spring/summer shows coming up, we need you, but I'm transferring you to Aisha's team." Dash had had enough of Jessica's unwanted advances. It was time to put an end to her constant flirting before her comments got out of hand.

Dash noticed the remorseful expression on Jessica's face before she turned around and returned to her cubicle.

Outside, Dash went next door to the drugstore and made a vital purchase, which he hoped to use before the night was over.

As the taxi drove along the West Side Highway, Dash reflected back on Lark's cold tone and how distant she seemed. *I hope she's not inviting me over to end things between us.*

The cab exited the highway and made its way down a tony block on Riverside Drive. Dash peered out of the window and marveled at the architecture of the prewar buildings. Having spent a significant amount of time in Europe, he had an appreciation for the craftsmanship of old structures. The car stopped at an eight-storied limestone building with ivory marble steps. He paid the fare and stepped out.

"Hello. I'm here to see Ms. Randolph," Dash told the doorman.

"Good evening. What's your name, sir?"

"Dash Migilio."

After the doorman rang Lark's apartment, he told Dash where to go. "Ms. Randolph is in penthouse A. Take the elevator to the left."

As Dash made his way through the ornate marble lobby toward the bank of elevators, he could feel a twinge of doubt creeping into his bones. There was a possibility that Lark would want nothing more to do with him. Dash slightly shook his head. He wasn't willing to believe this was the end of their brief love affair. He had much more to give, and he refused to go down without a fight.

The elevator arrived. He stepped on and pressed the button marked *PHA*. It didn't take long for the elevator to arrive at her floor. Dash's heart was pumping hard against his chest as he neared her penthouse. When he reached the door, it was ajar.

"Hello?" He spoke loudly and peeked his head in the door.

Dash didn't see Lark. He stepped in, closed the door and glanced around. Her living room was expertly decorated with two armless white leather sofas facing each other, a chocolate-brown suede shag rug between them. A huge abstract oil painting hung above the fireplace, and a crystal vase, filled with red ginger lilies, sat atop a mahogany baby grand piano.

"Sorry to keep you waiting. Please have a seat," Lark said, coming into the room, still wearing her work clothes.

Dash was too nervous to sit. He needed to speak his piece while he had the chance. "Lark, I think you saw my ex-girlfriend Heather in my office earlier today."

"I surely did." Lark was now seated on one of the sofas with her arms folded tightly across her chest.

"And I'm sure you saw her kiss me. I want you to know I did not return her kiss. Heather came to congratulate me on my new position, and she wanted to talk about getting back together."

Dash studied Lark's face, waiting for a reaction, but she just stared straight ahead with a stern look on her face. "I told her that wasn't going to happen because I'm in a relationship now."

"You said that?"

"Yes, I did. I also told her I'm a lucky man to be with

you. What we have is special, too special to be ruined by a misunderstanding."

Lark's lips parted into a slight smile. He could see he was breaking through her resolve, and he breathed a sigh of relief. Dash crossed the room, sat next to Lark, took her in his arms and kissed her softly. Initially, she felt tense in his embrace, until he turned up the heat, intensifying the kiss by sucking her bottom lip. He slipped his tongue into her mouth and swirled it around hers, and he didn't stop until she repeated the motions and their tongues were doing a sensuous duet.

"Wait a minute," Lark said, coming up for air. "Dash, maybe we should take a break. I've been lied to before, and I can't take any more deceit."

"Lark, I promise you my relationship with Heather is long over. You're the only woman I want."

"Dash, let's be honest. What we shared in Florence was wonderful, but it's over. Maybe you just wanted a fling with an older woman and I wanted one with a younger man. Now we're back in New York, let's concentrate on business. With the spring/summer shows quickly approaching, we can't afford to be distracted."

He reached into his messenger bag, took out a piece of paper and handed it to Lark. "First of all, I'm not distracted. This is a copy of the fax that Marco sent to customs this evening."

"I thought he wasn't going to be able to send it until tomorrow."

"After you spoke with Marco, I called again and had him expedite the paperwork so we can get the fabric as soon as possible."

"Thank you. I appreciate your diligence."

"There's no need to thank me. Like I told you before,

I want nothing more than for the new collection to be a success." Dash took Lark's hands in his. "And secondly, what we shared in Italy was definitely not a fling. I don't care about our age difference. I'm falling hard, Lark, and I want to be in a committed relationship with you."

"I don't know, Dash. Maybe we should slow things down."

"Why waste time? You can't deny the chemistry between us and I'm not just talking sexually. We work really well together, don't we?"

"Yes, we do."

Dash studied her face and could see a twinge of doubt in her eyes. "I can tell you're still unsure. Don't listen to your head. Listen to your heart."

Lark took a deep breath. "You're right. We do have great chemistry. If we are exclusive, that means your lips are reserved for only me…"

"I wouldn't have it any other way."

He covered her mouth with his, kissing her passionately. Dash began unbuttoning her blouse. He found the front clasp of her bra and unhooked it, allowing her breasts to fall free. Dash dusted her nipples with the palm of his hand before taking a mound of her breast in his hand. He massaged the soft tissue until her nipples began firming. He then leaned down and engulfed her right nipple in his mouth and started sucking, alternating with her left nipple.

While devouring her breasts, he eased his left hand down her leg and inched her skirt up so he could access her panties. When he felt the silky material, he slipped his fingers past the waistband and touched her smoothly shaven triangle. Dash found her clit and teased the tiny piece of flesh, which caused Lark to moan and squirm from his touch. He loved pleasing her and hearing her soft sounds of pleasure.

"Does that feel good?"

"Mmm...yes...it does."

Lark reached down and rubbed Dash's hardness through his pants. "You're getting excited."

"Yes, I am," he said.

Dash stopped, but only long enough to rise and retrieve the condoms he had brought. "Show me your bedroom," he said, reaching for her hand.

"Right this way." Lark took hold of his hand and led the way through the dining room, down a short hallway and into the master suite. The room was beautifully decorated with a king-size bed, a five-foot-tall white leather–quilted headboard, mirrored nightstands and lead-glass lamps.

Dash tossed the condoms on the nightstand and undressed down to his snug boxer briefs. He then watched as Lark slowly disrobed, giving him a strip show. After removing her blouse, she slipped off her bra. As he watched, he could feel his member getting firmer, until it was pressing hard against his underwear. She then unhooked her skirt and allowed it to fall to the floor. She stepped out of the garment and looked as if she was about to kick off her pumps.

"Keep your shoes on," he said in a sexy voice.

Lark struck a pose wearing just her purple lace thong and high heels. She put her hand on her hip. "You like what you see?"

"I surely do." Dash moved quickly in her direction. Within two steps, he was directly in front of her. He reached around and caressed her soft rear end, bringing her in closer. Dash kissed her neck as he rubbed his firmness against her. "You like what you feel?"

"Yes indeed," she said.

They stood in the middle of the floor, hugging and kissing like two people in love. Dash was becoming more aroused by the second and was finding it harder and harder to hold back.

"I want you in the worst way," he whispered in her ear.

"Not as bad as I want you," she said.

Dash took off his boxer briefs, reached for a condom, tore the wrapper and rolled the rubber onto his erectness. He then helped Lark out of her thong. "Turn around."

She turned, bent over and put her palms on the bed. Dash took her by the waist with one hand, gripped his member and smoothed it across her bare bottom. He was teasing her with each touch of his hardness.

Lark looked over her shoulder at Dash. "You are driving me crazy with desire. Please make love to me."

Her words were music to his ears. "I thought you'd never ask."

He slowly entered her from the back. Her sugar walls gripped him and held the length of him in place as they made love on the side of the bed, rocking against each other feverishly until they were nearly out of breath.

"You…you…feel…so good," he panted.

"Just don't stop!" she demanded.

Dash put one foot on the bed, pulled her in tighter and kicked up the pace. He was working the position to the best of his ability. Dash was pumping so hard he could feel a sheen of sweat on his back and down his chest. He kept going until their entire bodies were covered in perspiration. He reached down and licked the small of

Lark's back, tasting her salty sweat. He then took her by the hips, bringing her buttocks closer and closer. Lark's hands were now clenching the white duvet cover.

"Are you almost there yet?" he wanted to know.

"Yes! Yes! Yes!"

"Are you mine? Are you my lady?"

"Yes! Yes! Yes!" she screamed, beating her fists on the bed.

He pushed himself harder into her moistness, drilling her faster and faster, working like a human jackhammer. Dash felt himself coming and exploded into the condom.

"You're the best lover I've ever had," he said after catching his breath.

Lark fell onto the bed. "You're not so bad yourself," she teased.

"Not bad? Baby, I'm the best!"

After Dash disposed of the protection, he climbed into bed next to Lark and cradled her in his arms. Now that they were officially a couple, Dash didn't plan to ever let her go. She was his lover, and he would make sure nothing or no one stood in the way of their happiness.

Chapter 19

"Man, you've been MIA. I haven't seen or heard from you in weeks. What's going on with you?" Vance asked.

Dash was at Vance's Midtown law practice to sign papers regarding his annual charitable contribution, as well as other legal documents. It was his twenty-fifth birthday, which marked another hefty installment of his trust fund.

"Where should I start? I've been busy with work—I've been designing pieces to go in the collection for the upcoming show—*and* with my new lady."

"Wait a minute...new lady? The last time we had drinks, you were flying solo. Who is she?"

"Her name is Lark Randolph, and..."

"The COO of Randolph on the Runway?" Vance interrupted.

Dash smiled broadly at the mention of her name. "Yep, that's her."

"I've read about her in the press and have seen her picture. She's a knockout, but isn't she about ten years older than you?"

"I don't care how old she is. We're the perfect match, both professionally and personally. Lark is a grown woman and she knows what she wants. And so do I."

"When did all of this happen?" Vance asked, looking totally surprised. "Details. I want details."

"We flew to the mill in Florence because we needed them to produce a run of custom silks, and while we were there, we indulged in great food and wine. We soaked up the culture together. And for the short time we were there I got a chance to see a completely different side of Lark. The next thing you know, we were… uh…"

"In bed together?"

"That, too, but it's not just about the sex. We have a real connection, one I never had with Heather. Maybe Lark's maturity level makes her more grounded than the women I've dated in the past. Whatever it is, I'm sold. I can definitely see us having a long, fruitful future together."

"Man, sounds like you're ready to settle down."

"I am. Women like Lark don't come around every day, and I feel fortunate to have found her."

"Does she know you're a trust-fund baby who has enough money to buy a small country?"

"I briefly mentioned my trust fund, but didn't go into detail. Man, you know the money has never meant much to me. Don't misunderstand—it's nice to have a financial safety net in the event of an emergency. But my parents have always instilled in me that being a good, moral person and working hard count for more than multiple zeros in a bank account."

"It's true that money doesn't buy happiness, but it sure buys nice, expensive toys. Since it's your birthday, why don't you buy yourself a spiffy sports car?"

"I've already got one of those."

"Yeah, but it's in Florence. You need a dope ride here so I can borrow it sometimes," Vance said with a chuckle.

"Now, you know you have more than enough money to buy your own car."

"That's true, but I like investing my hard-earned cash instead so I can retire early. So what are you doing for the big two-five?"

"No plans. Maybe I'll take Lark to dinner. I haven't told her it's my birthday." Dash had never been one to make a big fuss over his birthday. Unlike most people, he preferred to treat the day like any other.

"Well, you have plans now. I'm going to call a few friends and invite them out tonight. I refuse to let another one of your milestone birthdays pass without a celebration."

"What's the use in trying to say no? Vance, I know when you get an idea in your head, there's no stopping you. So where are we going?"

"The 40/40 Club. I have a connection there and should be able to reserve one of their private rooms at the last minute. Hold on—let me make a call."

Vance picked up his office phone and dialed the private number to the club. "Hey, man, it's Vance…I'm good. Listen, I was wondering if there are any suites available for tonight?…Okay, great. Thanks." He disconnected the line. "We're in. Let's meet at eight."

"Okay, sounds good. Now back to business."

Vance handed Dash a few documents that were flagged for his signature. After Dash signed the paperwork, he stood and said, "See you tonight, and thanks for making the arrangements for my party."

"No problem."

On his way back home, Dash started warming up to the idea of having a celebration. It would give him an opportunity to introduce Lark to some of his friends. He took out his cell phone and called her.

"Hey, babe, how are you?"

"I'm good. I was just thinking about you."

"Naughty thoughts, I hope."

"How did you know?"

"I can read your mind?"

"I knew you were a gifted designer, but I had no idea you were clairvoyant."

"Babe, I have many talents," he said with a chuckle. "Wait a minute… I'm getting a vibe that you don't have plans for tonight."

"Wrong. I was thinking about ordering a pizza and watching an old black-and-white movie. You want to come over so we can act out my naughty thoughts?"

"We'll do that after the party tonight," he said, full of excitement.

"Whose party are we going to?"

"Mine. Today is my birthday and my friend Vance is organizing a small get-together at the 40/40 Club."

"Happy birthday, honey! Why didn't you mention this before? I would have planned a special evening for us."

"I usually don't make a big deal about my birthday, but today is my twenty-fifth, so Vance thought I should celebrate."

"He's absolutely right! You're only twenty-five once. What time should I meet you there?"

"I'll pick you up at seven-thirty."

"Okay, see you then."

After hanging up, he called his driver and arranged a pickup. He then stopped in an exclusive grooming boutique that catered to men for some facial products before heading home.

Before long, day had wound down to evening and Dash was showered, shaved, dressed and ready to pick up his lover. He took one last look in the floor-length mirror in his bathroom, approving of his black Burberry shirt and tapered black slacks. Dash slapped his face with aftershave, turned off the light and left.

Downstairs, his car and driver, which he rarely used, was waiting curbside in front of his condo building. Dash instructed the driver on where to go. The car cut through traffic, snaked up Riverside Drive and stopped in front of Lark's building.

Dash took out his phone and called Lark. "Hey, babe, I'm downstairs."

"I'll be right down."

Moments later, Lark strutted out of the building. Dash immediately stepped out and opened the door for her. He did a slow whistle as he took in her appearance. She wore a snug black dress with a flared peplum at the waist and a pair of black rhinestone stilettos that clicked along the pavement as she made her way to the car. Her hair was pinned back, showcasing her princess-cut diamond studs. And her makeup was flawless.

"I guess it's Code Black tonight. You look stunning," he said, greeting her with a kiss on the lips.

"Thank you, and you look handsome yourself." Lark gave him a kiss on the lips. "Happy birthday, baby."

Once they settled in the backseat, Dash retrieved a bottle of champagne from a mini cooler. He popped the cork, poured them each a glass and suggested a toast.

"Here's to spending this birthday and every day hereafter together."

"I'll drink to that." Lark smiled broadly. "Had you told me earlier that it was your birthday, I would have gotten you a gift. I'm just going to have to think of some other way to celebrate with you." She moved closer and whispered, "Is there a window to separate us from the driver so we can have a little privacy?" she asked, resting her hand on his thigh.

"There sure is." Dash pressed a button, and instantaneously a thick plate of glass sprang up in front of them, sealing off the driver.

"Now, that's better." Lark moved her hand up Dash's leg and began seductively kneading his private area. His mound of flesh was lax until she increased the pressure, giving him a firm yet gentle rubdown. She unbuckled his belt, then unbuttoned and unzipped his pants. "I see somebody's getting excited."

"See what you do to me?"

"I'm going to do more than that. Just you wait."

Lark found the opening to his black boxer briefs and reached her hand in. She took her left hand and held his shaft as she kissed the head. Lark then engulfed the full length of him in her mouth, alternating between sucking and licking. She peered up at Dash. His head was laid back on the seat and his eyes were closed. Lark stopped suddenly and waited.

"Why…why'd you stop?" he asked, seemingly in a daze.

"Just wanted to make sure you're enjoying your present."

"Oh, yeah! It's the best gift ever."

Lark didn't say another word. She resumed her expert technique, only this time with extra force.

Dash placed his hands on her head and rode the wave of pleasure. He found the unexpected "gift" totally erotic. He loved her spontaneity. She was exciting him more and more with each touch of her mouth.

"Damn, baby, you've got skills, but let's save this until after the party."

"Are you sure?" she asked, coming up for air.

"Yes, but don't worry—we'll definitely pick up where we left off. You are something else, Lark Randolph. You're full of surprises."

"I just like pleasing my man," Lark said, a mischievous grin on her face.

Chapter 20

As the Mercedes arrived at the 40/40 Club, Lark noticed a group of young women scantily clad in short shorts, midriff tops that revealed their bellies and heels so tall they resembled small stilts. They were posing behind a velvet rope like supermodels in training, waiting to gain entry into the trendy nightspot. Lark had never been to this bar, and she wondered if the clientele was too young for her liking. Those in line seemed to barely be over the drinking age. Suddenly, she felt old, overdressed and out of place.

Why did his friend pick this place? Looks like the people going in still have breast milk on their breath. "I think I should go back home and let you and your friends enjoy the party. This isn't my scene."

Dash took her by the hand. "There's no way I'm letting you leave. Yes, the crowd does look young, but Vance reserved a private room. Come on. It'll be fun."

She exhaled. "Oh...okay."

They exited the car and moved past the velvet rope. Dash gave the menacing-looking doorman his name, and they were ushered inside.

Lark took a look around at the chicly designed, cavernous space, with its muted tones of gray. The focal point of the room was a towering display featuring golden bottles of champagne. The crowd outside may have been young, but the interior design of the club was mature and laid-back.

A hostess greeted them and led the way through the main level, up an open flight of stairs, to the top floor, where the private rooms were located. She opened one of many doors. Inside was a richly appointed sports-themed suite with large framed pictures of Babe Ruth, Jackie Robinson, Michael Jordan, Larry Bird and Magic Johnson, among others. A black felt-covered pool table occupied the center of the space.

The first thing Lark noticed after entering the room was the ratio of women to men. There were at least three females to every male. It was obvious a guy had organized the party and had invited more women than men. The entire group seemed to be under thirty. Lark self-consciously tugged at the peplum on her dress, now wishing she had worn something more casual, like leggings and a leather jacket, instead of a dinner outfit. *Oh well, there's nothing I can do about it now,* she thought and stopped fidgeting with her clothes.

"There's the birthday boy!" Vance said, excusing himself from a group of women and walking toward Dash with his arms wide open. After hugging his friend, Vance turned to Lark. "And you must be Lark Randolph." He lifted her hand and kissed the top of it.

"Hey, man, don't be kissing my girlfriend," Dash teased.

Lark watched the handsome men and could just imagine them giving the ladies double trouble. Vance, with his rich chocolate skin and closely cropped hair, was just as striking as Dash. He was dressed to the nines, in a purple-and-white-striped shirt, purple tie, gray vest and slacks.

"Sorry, man, my bad!" Vance threw his hands up in mock surrender.

"Nice to meet you, Vance," Lark said.

"You guys are a few drinks behind and need to catch up. Let me get you some champagne," Vance offered, walking over to the bar area. After pouring the bubbly, he gave them each a glass and then gave a toast. "To Dash, one of my favorite people. May you have many more healthy, happy birthdays!"

"I'll drink to that." Dash clinked his glass to theirs and downed his champagne in two swallows.

"Happy birthday, baby!" Lark said, chiming in. "So how long have you two been friends?"

"Since high school, Dash was always the goody-goody boy. He didn't have a string of girlfriends and always made it home before curfew," Vance said, laughing.

"What was wrong with dating one girl at a time and obeying the house rules?" Dash responded.

"Absolutely nothing," Lark said, jumping in. She could tell by Vance's cavalier attitude, he was the playboy type. Although Vance seemed like a nice guy, Lark was glad Dash didn't share his friend's viewpoint.

Dash kissed Lark on the mouth. "Thank you, babe, for coming to my defense."

"Anytime, love. You know I got your back."

"Aw…you two are just too mushy," Vance said, waving his hand in their direction.

"It's not mushy. It's called *a relationship,*" Dash said, correcting his friend.

"I hear you, man. Maybe one day I'll be lucky enough to find the right woman to settle down with," Vance said with a serious tone to his voice.

"Hey there, handsome. Remember me?" a woman asked Dash as she approached them.

"Uh…not really," Dash responded.

Lark eyed the short woman with the long weave. She was wearing heavy makeup and a tight hot-pink dress with a plunging neckline that exposed balloon-type breasts.

"Me and Cindy—" she pointed across the room to another woman "—were at the Monkey Bar and tried to buy you guys a drink. Vance stayed, but you left before we had a chance to meet."

"Oh, yeah," Dash responded.

"You should have stayed. The three of us had a great time that night," she said without shame.

"That we did." Vance leaned closer to Dash and whispered, "I finally got my threesome and it was awesome."

"Good for you," Dash whispered back.

"Come on, Dash. Let me introduce you to Cindy. She's dying to meet you," the woman said, totally ignoring Lark.

"No disrespect, but I'm here with my girlfriend." He took Lark by the waist and pulled her to his side.

The short woman gave Lark an up-and-down look.

"Oh…my bad. I didn't know you were taken."

"Yes, I am," Dash responded, hugging Lark even closer.

Lark couldn't believe the gall of the woman, talking

to Dash as if she weren't standing there. Lark had the mind to set her straight, but thankfully Dash had already done so. Lark was relieved to know her man wasn't the type of guy who flirted openly with other women in her presence.

"You got some tequila behind the bar? I've had enough champagne," the woman said to Vance.

"Anything for you, baby. Let's go downstairs and get a bottle. We'll be right back," Vance said, escorting the woman out of the room.

"So is this what I have to look forward to?" Lark asked.

"What do you mean?"

"Women coming out of the woodwork to pour themselves all over you."

"What can I say? I'm hot!" Dash laughed.

Lark didn't crack a smile. "I'm not kidding, Dash. You're a chick magnet, and honestly, I don't know if I want to deal with all the competition." Lark spoke her mind without any filters. Seeing Dash in a group of his peers brought home the fact that they ran in completely different social circles. He would always be on the radar of young, brazen women.

Dash held Lark in his arms and kissed her with abandon. "I couldn't care less about other women, young or old. I'm committed to you. You got that?" he asked, releasing her.

"Yes."

"Good. Now, I don't want to hear any more doubts or age-related comments," he said in a stern voice.

Lark knew Dash was being truthful. He only had eyes for her. The lingering doubts she'd had about them were now gone. Lark realized that if they were to have a successful relationship, she would have to release all negative thoughts about the two of them. Their age difference was something she could never change, but she could change her outlook on the matter. She vowed from here on out not to revisit the issue, since Dash had firmly put her fears to rest.

When Vance returned with a bottle of Corzo Anejo, he poured shots for the four of them. "Happy birthday, my friend!"

Lark sipped her shot of tequila, while everyone else downed theirs.

"Wait a minute—we're doing shots, not sips!" Vance said to Lark.

"I can't possibly drink all of this in one gulp."

"Maybe you need a wedge of lime and some salt," Vance said, handing Lark the chasers.

"Here, let me show you how I do it," the woman said. She squeezed lime juice in her mouth followed by a sprinkling of salt. She then downed another shot.

"Okay, your turn," Vance said, nudging Lark's elbow.

Lark did exactly as the woman had done. She wrinkled her nose and shook her head after swallowing the liquor.

"Are you okay, babe?" Dash asked.

She nodded her head. "That wasn't too bad… Let me have another shot," Lark responded.

"That's what I'm talking about!" Vance said and poured another round.

They spent the remainder of the evening doing shots and playing pool. Lark had entered the 40/40 Club with trepidation, but she was now having the time of her life.

"Come here, you," she said, nearly slurring her words.

Lark tugged on Dash's collar after he had finished playing a game of pool with Vance.

"Looks like somebody is having a good time," he said.

"I'm having a ball, but I could be having an even better time."

"Oh, yeah? What would make this party better?" he asked.

Lark peered around the room. Into his ear, she whispered, "Is there a private restroom?"

Dash nodded his head in the direction of the far wall. "Yep, right over there."

"Okay, I'm going to go in first and then you're going to come in after me. Understood?"

"Yes, ma'am!"

Lark disappeared behind a door. The bathroom was just as plush as the main suite, with a sitting area, a marble sink and a huge framed mirror. Lark leaned against the sink, hiked up her dress and removed her thong. She struck a pose looking over her shoulder in the mirror at her naked butt. Ever since she had been with Dash, Lark found herself doing and saying things she had never done before. Instead of shying away from the new adventures, she was embracing them.

"Wow! Look at you!" Dash said in a hushed tone, stepping into the bathroom and locking the door behind him.

"What can I say? I hope you have a condom, because I'm ready to get my groove on."

Dash retrieved his wallet from his pocket and produced a gold-wrapped rubber. He walked behind Lark, put the package on the counter and took two handfuls of her buttocks. "Babe, you are so hot!"

Lark jutted her butt out farther. "Thank you," she said.

"I'm truly a lucky man."

Dash unzipped his pants, reached into the opening and removed his member. "I want you," he whispered in her ear. Dash then ripped the foil wrapper, took out the condom and rolled it onto his slate-hard manhood. "Lean over."

Lark placed her hands on the counter, arched her back and readied herself for her lover.

Dash eased the tip of his manhood into her wetness, took her by the hips and began slowly rotating inside her. He moved his member around and around, circling her moistness.

"Ohh, that feels so good," Lark whispered.

Dash held her tighter and filled her moist insides. He was holding and lifting Lark off her feet with each determined thrust.

Lark held on to the counter and clinched her eyes shut. He felt so good inside of her that she wanted to scream out in pleasure, but she kept silent as Dash took her from behind. She opened her eyes and watched the two of them in the mirror. The sight of her and Dash making love was so erotic that she let ecstasy take over and gave in to her desires. Soon after, Lark could feel Dash slowing down. He gave a few more hard pushes and reached the pinnacle shortly after she did.

"Happy birthday, baby!"

Chapter 21

Lark was sitting at her drafting table. She should have been working on sketches for their fall/winter line, but her head was pounding and she was finding it difficult to concentrate. She had a major headache, a result of drinking too much tequila the night before. Dash's twenty-fifth birthday celebration had gone on until last call was announced. By then, they had polished off two bottles of tequila and quite a few bottles of champagne. Lark hadn't partied like that since her early thirties. Being with a younger man had its perks—great sex—and its pitfalls—staying out too late on a work night.

She rose from the stool and went over to her desk for a bottle of aspirin. She swallowed three small white pills with a sip of water. Lark sat down, put her head in her hands and began massaging her temples, trying to alleviate the pain.

"Looks like somebody has a hangover."

Lark slowly raised her head. Dash was standing in the doorway looking fresh and spry, as if he hadn't tied one on the night before. His navy pin-striped suit fit his body perfectly. His white shirt was neatly laundered, his hair coiffed and his face smoothly shaven.

"As a matter of fact, I do. How's your head?"

"Fine. I feel great!" He walked into her office and sat in one of the chairs facing her.

"You're all starched and pressed. Where did you go this morning? When I woke up, you were gone."

They had ended the night back at his place, where Lark had passed out across the bed with her clothes still on. She had crept past his doorman, made it home, showered, changed and barely made it to the office before nine.

"I had a meeting with the president of the Boys and Girls Club of America. They are one of the organizations I sponsor annually. I donate funds every year after my birthday. It's a tradition I started after my inheritance kicked in when I was sixteen."

Lark smiled despite her throbbing headache. Dash was young, but he had admirable qualities. "That's sweet of you to give back. I'm sure they appreciate your generosity."

"Yes, they do. I'd rather help those less fortunate than waste money on useless games at a casino or a fleet of luxury cars."

"Dash Migilio, you are a wise soul. I think you've been on this Earth before," she said with a chuckle.

"That's what my mother always tells me. I'm not so wise. I just believe in doing the right thing. Not to sound boastful, but I have enough money to last a few lifetimes. I'd rather share my good fortune than have it sitting in a bank."

As they were talking, Angelica came into the office. "Here's your mail," she said, giving Lark a stack of envelopes, large and small.

"Thanks, and, Angelica, can you order me a double shot of espresso?"

"Sure. Dash, would you like anything from the coffee shop?" Angelica asked.

"No, thanks."

Once Angelica left, Lark took a letter opener from her desk drawer and began ripping open the envelopes one at a time.

"So tell me, Dash, why don't you have a hangover? I feel like a truck broadsided me."

"The key is water. I tried to get you to drink a bottle of water, but you kept yelling, 'Shot, shot, shot!'"

"I vaguely remember that."

"Maybe next time you'll listen to me."

"I promise you there won't be a next time. I'll stick to my Manhattans. Those I can handle."

"You drink Manhattans? So do I. That's my dad's favorite cocktail. He started drinking them when he moved to New York. He always said that he was living in Manhattan, so he might as well drink one."

"That's a cute story."

"Do you want to go out to dinner tonight? There's a new restaurant in the Village I want to take you to."

Lark didn't respond. She was holding a check in her hand and reading the accompanying note. "Oh, no!" she blurted out.

"What's wrong?"

"I can't believe this!"

"What?"

"It's a check from one of the major retailers, but it's short by seventy thousand dollars!"

"Why?"

"The letter says they deducted funds for markdowns in order to put our merchandise on sale," she said in disbelief.

"Why didn't they notify you beforehand?"

"I don't know. I usually get an email well in advance of them deducting markdown money." Lark tossed the letter on the desk and slumped back in her chair. "I can't believe this!"

"Maybe it's a mistake. Why don't you give the buyer a call?"

"Yes, she could have mixed up our sales numbers with those of another vendor."

Lark searched the contact file on her computer and found the buyer's number. She reached for the phone and made the call.

"Patricia Taylor speaking."

"Hi, Pat, it's Lark Randolph over at Randolph on the Runway."

"Hi, Lark, what can I do for you?"

"I'm calling to clear up a misunderstanding. I just received a check from your store from our last purchase order, but it's short seventy thousand dollars."

"Hold on a second. Let me check our records." After a brief pause, she came back on the line. "There's no misunderstanding. That number is correct—we made the adjustment to account for the markdown money. The collection wasn't moving, so we had to reduce the prices."

"Why didn't you send me a notification email?" Lark asked.

"I did. Sebastian received the email. He knew about the markdowns well in advance of the check going out."

Lark was shocked to hear this news. She had already earmarked that money for expenditures and had no idea that Sebastian had been in contact with the buyer. "When did you talk to him?"

"Let me check the date on the email." The buyer gave Lark the exact date and time of the email.

"Why did you email Sebastian? Normally those notices come directly to me."

"Sebastian called to get an update on sales, and we spoke at length about how the line just wasn't selling as well as we'd anticipated. As a matter of fact, he insisted that we deduct the markdown money from the invoice. I was prepared to give the line more time to move, but Sebastian was adamant about the reduction. He told me he would forward you the information. Is there a problem?"

"Not at all. Thanks for clarifying everything, Pat. Talk to you soon." Lark wasn't about to go into detail about how she thought her former lead designer was trying to sabotage her company. The buyer would probably be full of questions. Lark didn't want rumors floating around in the industry that RR was in financial trouble. She disconnected the line and exhaled hard in despair.

"I can't believe this! That dirty son of a…"

"What's going on?" Dash asked, scooting to the edge of his chair.

"Sebastian pulled a fast one on his last day. He purposely didn't tell me about the markdowns. He knew full well I would be thrown off guard once I received this abbreviated check. Sebastian and I had even talked about how the funds from the order that Pat placed would help with the production of the new collection. Now the company's short seventy grand. I was really counting on that check." Lark picked up a pencil and tapped the eraser on her desk. She was trying to think of a solution to her financial deficit, but nothing came to mind.

"Don't look so forlorn. It's not that bad."

"Trust me. It is that bad. I'm going to have to pull some pieces from the collection. We can't afford to produce them all."

"You'll do nothing of the sort."

"It's either pull pieces from the line or lay someone off. I have no choice. After I pay the vendors, there won't be much left."

Dash stood up, took his checkbook out of his breast pocket and sat back down. He reached for a pen on her desk, wrote out a check, ripped it out of the book and handed it to Lark. "Here you go. Problem solved."

Lark took the check and read the amount. "I can't take a hundred thousand dollars from you." She tried to hand the check back, but Dash wouldn't take it.

"You can and you will. It's only money, and there's plenty more where that came from. I refuse to see all of your hard work go down the drain over money. Take the check and call it a grant if it makes you feel better."

"Dash, how can I ever repay you?"

"You don't repay a grant."

Lark felt tears well up in her eyes. She had never experienced this type of generosity before. "Thank you, Dash."

"You're welcome. Now let me get back to work." He leaned over and kissed her on the forehead.

Once Dash was gone, Lark stood and walked over to the window. She looked to the azure-blue sky and said a silent prayer of thanks. Dash was a miracle, not only personally, but professionally, and she could not have asked for a better partner in life.

Chapter 22

Dash didn't like seeing Lark in despair. He wanted to wring Sebastian's neck for being so deceitful. If Dash knew where to find the guy, he would have gone and confronted him face-to-face. Since that wasn't a choice, he did the next best thing. Instead of going to his office to work on new designs, he left the building to run an important errand.

Once outside, he hailed a taxi and told the driver to take him to 299 Park Avenue. The yellow cab whizzed across town through the midmorning traffic. Along the way, Dash made a call to his private banker.

"Hi there, Hans. I hope you can squeeze me in this morning. I need to take care of a pressing matter. It shouldn't take long."

"Good morning, Dash. Of course I have time for you. When should I expect you?"

"I'm on my way. See you in a few," Dash said and disconnected the call.

He knew it wouldn't be a problem seeing the banker on such short notice. Dash was one of the bank's premier clients. He usually didn't throw his weight around, making spur-of-the-moment demands, but this was urgent and couldn't wait until the following day.

When the taxi arrived in front of the bank, Dash paid the driver, got out and went directly to the private-banking floor.

"Good morning, Mr. Migilio," the receptionist greeted him. "Would you care for a cup of coffee or a Danish?"

"No, thanks, Ellen." Dash had been a client for years and was on a first-name basis with all of the employees.

"Mr. Oppenheim is expecting you. He's in his office."

"Thank you." Dash walked down the hallway with urgency. He didn't have time to waste—he was on a mission.

"Dash, what brings you by this morning?" Hans asked, reaching his hand out and shaking Dash's.

Dash shook the banker's hand and took a seat. "I need to move some money and set up a line of credit."

"How much are you talking about?"

"Five hundred to start with. That should be sufficient."

"Five thousand dollars?" the banker asked.

"No, five hundred thousand."

Hans looked shocked. "A half a million dollars? That's a lot of money, Dash."

"Yes, I know," he said casually.

"You just came into your inheritance. Why do you need the extra cash now, if I may ask?"

"I want to start a line of credit for Randolph on the

Runway. The company is up against some financial challenges and I want to have funds ready and available when they are needed."

"Do you think it's wise to invest your personal money in a company you work for? Have you ever thought about starting your own company?" the older man asked with a concerned expression.

"That's not my focus at the moment. Besides, Randolph on the Runway isn't just any company. I have a vested interest in its success." Dash didn't want to divulge his personal connection to Lark. One, it wasn't the banker's business, and two, he didn't have to explain why he chose to spend his money the way he did.

"Oh, I see. Okay. I'll draw up the paperwork now." Hans went to work on his computer and before long printed out a document. "Initial here and here, and sign here," he said, pointing to the designated areas.

Dash authorized the papers, giving his consent to transfer funds from an investment account into a separate account for Randolph on the Runway. He knew if he had told Lark what he was planning, she would have probably forbidden him from doing so. Dash could see she'd had a hard time accepting the check, and he could only imagine what her reaction would be to a half-a-million-dollar line of credit.

The launch of the new collection was getting closer, and with Sebastian on the loose, there was no telling what else the guy had up his sleeve. It was clear to Dash the former employee was disgruntled and was out for revenge. Dash didn't know what was coming down the pike, but he knew having sufficient funds available would come in handy if necessary.

"Thanks, Hans, for expediting this matter. I really appreciate it."

"No problem, Dash. That's what I'm here for." Hans give Dash a folder with copies of the documents. "Take care."

On Dash's way back to work, he phoned a private chef whom he used occasionally and asked him to prepare a gourmet meal for two later that evening. The chef had a key and clearance to enter Dash's penthouse when he wasn't there. Lark was having a trying day, but Dash planned on making her evening much better.

"Where have you been?" Lark asked the second Dash stepped off the elevator. She was coming down the hallway from a meeting and nearly bumped into him. "You missed Aisha's presentation. She tweaked some of her designs for the collection, and I wanted your feedback."

"I'm sorry. I forgot all about the meeting. I had an important errand to run. I'll go by her office and see what changes she's made."

"Okay. I have to jump on a conference call with one of our Asian vendors. See you later," Lark said and sped off down the hall.

Dash went in the opposite direction toward Aisha's office. Jessica was standing outside of her new cubicle when he walked up.

"Hello, Dash," she said in a professional voice.

"Hey there. How are you settling in over here?" he asked. Dash looked at Jessica's outfit—for once she was dressed appropriately in a pair of black slacks, a blazer and a jacket.

"Really well. I like working with Aisha. She's shown me a lot in a short period of time. She's a good teacher."

"Good." Dash could see through the plate glass that

Aisha wasn't in her office. "Do you know when she will be back?"

"She went downstairs to see the patternmakers. Do you want me to have her call you when she gets back?"

"Yes, that'll be great," Dash said, and then he walked away. He was relieved Jessica was no longer trying to flirt with him. After the debacle with Heather, he didn't need any more drama at work. He and Lark were on steady ground, and he planned to keep it that way.

Dash busied himself for the rest of the day, sketching new designs for upcoming seasons and working on a line of handbags that could possibly help expand the business into leather goods. He hadn't spoken to Lark about this new idea yet. She was under so much pressure surrounding the spring/summer collection that he decided to wait until the shows were over.

By the time Dash had finished working, it was well after business hours and most of the employees had gone for the day. He stood, stretched and walked down to Lark's office.

"Hey, you. Are you ready to call it a night?"

Lark was staring at her computer screen. "Not yet. I want to plug the rest of these numbers into the spreadsheet before I leave."

"Can't that wait until tomorrow? We've both had a long day. Come on—let's go home," he said from where he stood in the doorway.

"Well…I guess I could do this tomorrow. Let me log off. I'll meet you by the elevators."

"Okay."

Dash went back to his office and called the chef to make sure everything was on schedule. "How's it going?"

"Everything is ready. Do you want me to stay?" the chef asked.

"No, you don't have to. I think I can manage to put the food on plates," Dash said with a chuckle. He hung up, gathered his messenger bag and headed for the elevators.

"I'm starving," Lark told him on their way down to the lobby.

"That makes two of us."

"Where do you want to go for dinner?" she asked. "What about that new Mexican place around the corner?"

"We'll try them some other time. Let's go to my place for dinner instead."

Lark looked at him out of the side of her eye. "Can you cook? Or are we going to order in?"

"No takeout tonight. Let's just say I know how to orchestrate a good meal."

The moment Lark stepped into Dash's penthouse, she caught the aroma of rosemary and citrus. She took a deep whiff. "Hmm, something sure smells good!"

"Let's go into the kitchen and see what the chef has whipped up."

"You have a chef?"

"Not on a regular basis. I only call him when I want a special meal prepared. I thought since we've both been working hard, we would stay in tonight and enjoy a good meal and relax."

They went into the gourmet kitchen. Everything was white, from the quartz countertops to the ceiling-high cabinets—even the appliances were white. The entire space looked like a page out of *Architectural Digest*.

"I love your kitchen," Lark said, glancing around.

"I'll tell my mother you said so. She designed the space after I moved in. I told her I didn't need all these high-end appliances, but she insisted, saying that when I got married my wife would appreciate a nice kitchen."

"That was thoughtful of her. I for one rarely use my kitchen. I'm not home enough to cook on a regular basis."

"That makes two of us. That's why I have the number to an amazing chef. What have we here?" Dash said, going over to the eight-burner range. He lifted the lid off a roaster pan. "He made baked chicken with rosemary and lemon with baby vegetables." He opened the oven, took out a dish and removed the glass top. "And macaroni and cheese."

"Yum, I love comfort food! What a treat!"

"Glad you approve." Dash removed his blazer, washed his hands, took plates out of the cabinet and dished up their meals. He put the plates on the counter, and they wasted no time digging in.

Lark was speechless as she devoured her food. She hadn't eaten much all day, and she was enjoying the delicious treat. "That was so tasty," she said, wiping the corners of her mouth with a napkin.

"Would you like seconds?"

"I shouldn't, but…why not?"

Dash refilled her plate and his, cleaning the roaster of its contents.

"Tell your chef he can cook for me anytime," Lark commented after she polished off the last of the macaroni and cheese.

"Will do. Would you like a glass of wine?"

"No, thank you. Having finally gotten rid of my tequila headache, I need a break from alcohol for the next few days. Water will be just fine."

Dash reached in the refrigerator and took out two bottles of water. "Let's go into the living room and relax," Dash said, leading the way.

Lark kicked off her shoes and settled on the oversize sofa while Dash put on a smooth-jazz CD. When he returned to the couch, she snuggled up next to him. "Thanks so much for such a wonderful meal. This was exactly what I needed."

"You're quite welcome. You want to watch a movie?"

"No, thanks. I just want to sit here and listen to the music. It sounds so soothing." Lark closed her eyes and was soon in a Zenlike state. She was totally satiated. The day had started off rocky, but now everything had mellowed out, thanks to Dash. Her mind was free from the stress of work, and she drifted off to sleep with ease.

Chapter 23

Lark had fallen asleep on Dash's sofa, but she was jolted awake by the sound of her own light snoring. Dash had been asleep next to her. He was sleeping so soundly that she hadn't wanted to disturb him, so she'd quietly put on her shoes, gathered her things and headed home before midnight. She had wanted to sleep in her own bed in order to get a good night's rest. Now, early in the morning, she was refreshed and ready to face the day.

Lark was sitting in her kitchen, dressed in a terry-cloth robe, drinking a cup of freshly brewed hazelnut coffee. Her tablet was propped up on the counter next to her. Instead of reading the *New York Times,* she was perusing the daily fashion blogs to catch up on the latest news. She had been so inundated with her own designs that she hadn't taken the time to check out what the other designers were creating. With fashion week approaching, she wanted to check out the competition. Lark normally stayed on top of the latest happenings, but with dating Dash and her heavy work schedule, she had fallen behind. Lark was scanning the page of Iman M, a hot young fashion stylist and blogger who reported on the latest trends on Seventh Avenue before, during and after the fashion shows. Iman had written...

An Old Face with a New Look. Sebastian (no last name required), former lead designer of Randolph on the Runway, has launched his own line. His new womenswear collection is fresh and exciting. I'll be at his Tribeca loft this afternoon for a sneak peek before fashion week starts. I'll be posting pix of Sebastian's new line on my page. Ciao!

"Sebastian's preview, huh? I'll be there, as well," Lark said aloud. She was curious to see what her former employee had been up to since his firing. Lark knew exactly where Sebastian's loft was located—she had been there numerous times for his quaint cocktail parties.

Lark dressed for the day in a slate-gray jumpsuit with an asymmetrical collar—another of her latest designs—and a thin gunmetal belt around her slim waist. She headed to the office. When she arrived, her assistant was sitting at her desk.

"Good morning, Ms. Randolph. Here's your mail." Angelica handed her a stack of envelopes.

"Thanks." Lark took the pile of mail and headed inside her office. She dropped the mail on her desk and scanned through it. She could see from the envelopes that some of them were bills. She put them to the side and logged on to her computer. There was a slew of new emails—some professional and some personal—that she hadn't read yet. Lark knew she should open and answer them, but she couldn't concentrate. Her mind was on Sebastian. She couldn't stop thinking about the way he had purposely left her in the dark about the markdown money. Lark planned to show up at his loft and give him a piece of her mind.

After forcing herself to focus, she finished plugging numbers into the spreadsheet she had been working on the day before. Even though it wasn't noon yet, she decided to head over to Sebastian's to get their unpleasant exchange over with. She wanted to confront him before the blogger arrived.

"Angelica, I'm leaving for a while. I should be back in an hour or two," she said.

"Don't forget you have a meeting with production at three," Angelica said.

"I'll be back before then."

On her way to the elevator, she looked around the office and saw Dash was sitting at his drafting table, wielding his pencil. Whatever he was working on, she didn't want to interrupt his flow, so she kept stepping without disturbing him. If he had known she was on her way to see Sebastian, Lark was sure Dash would want to come with her. She didn't need his help this time. Lark had no problem having a face-to-face confrontation with Sebastian.

Outside, Lark hailed a taxi and headed downtown. On the way there, she ran different scenarios through her mind. Would she and Sebastian get into a screaming match like they had the last time they were together? Or would they have a civil exchange, wherein she could ask him why he had tried to sabotage a company he had once been so dedicated to? She reasoned he had acted out of anger from being fired without notice. Lark wanted to speak her mind and make peace with Sebastian. She thought that since some time had gone by, they could come to a mutual admiration for each other. After all, they had worked closely together. Since they were in the same industry, they were bound to run into each other. Lark didn't want any bad blood with him.

The driver stopped in front of a warehouselike building on Reade Street. She got out of the taxi, and as she made her way to the front door, Lark's heart began beating a bit faster. *Maybe I should have asked Dash to come along,* she thought, second-guessing her decision to go alone. Lark took a deep breath to calm herself and found Sebastian's name and unit number on the bell panel near the door, pushed the button and waited for him to respond. She heard a buzzing sound on the other end of the intercom. She pushed open the door and went inside.

The small, plain hallway was free of any frills. It had an old gated elevator and an antique staircase to the right. Lark knew from past experience the elevator could be temperamental. She weighed her options. *Should I take the elevator and chance getting stuck or walk up three flights of steps?* She decided on the latter.

When she reached his floor, she was out of breath. *I really need to get back to the gym.* Lark walked down the long corridor with her heels clicking on the wood plank floor. Sebastian's door was ajar, but she knocked anyway.

"Come on in!" he shouted.

Lark took a deep breath and stepped inside. She looked around, expecting to see Sebastian in all of his flamboyant glory, but he was nowhere in sight. There were Andy Warhol prints of Marilyn Monroe and Liz Taylor on the whitewashed brick walls. Sebastian had bragged during one of his infamous cocktail parties that he and Andy had danced together at Studio 54 back during the disco days. And that Andy had personally given him the signed prints, which were some of his most prized possessions.

A group of nude female mannequins were standing around waiting to be clothed. Lark noticed new additions to his loft: a sewing area with six industrial machines, a six-foot-long drafting table and bolts of fabric. Obviously Sebastian was producing garments out of his residence, which she found interesting.

"You're early, Iman. I'll be right out," he said with a lilt to his voice.

Oh, he thinks I'm that blogger. Lark didn't respond. She wanted to surprise him like he had surprised her with the markdowns. She moseyed around the space, trying to see signs of what Sebastian was working on, but there was nothing in sight, no spools of thread on the machines or remnants of material on the floor.

"Okay, it's showtime!" Sebastian announced loudly from the back.

Lark turned toward the sound of his voice and waited for him to appear. He did not. Instead, a string of models strutted through a doorway draped in black velvet, wearing long, billowy dresses, jumpsuits with wide legs and pencil-leg slack pantsuits. Lark felt weak in the knees as she watched the mini fashion show unfold.

The models paraded around the loft and then struck poses in the middle of the floor. Shortly thereafter, Sebastian entered wearing a male version of one of the jumpsuits.

"So, Ms. Scott, how do you like—" He stopped mid-sentence when he saw Lark. "What the hell are you doing here?"

"No. The question is, where the hell did you get my designs from?" Lark approached one of the models and inspected the garment she was wearing. "That jumpsuit is exactly like the one I have on, except the fabric is different!"

"So what?" he snapped.

"It's from the new collection. A collection that hasn't even gone into production yet. I'm wearing the only sample piece." As Lark spoke, her mind flashed back to the computer breach at the company that had caused all of their files to be wiped out. "You…you broke into our system and stole the designs!"

Sebastian casually rolled his eyes. He looked at his manicured nails and said, "Prove it!"

Lark was fuming mad. She was tempted to pick up one of his large coffee-table books and throw it at him, but she maintained her composure. She didn't need any witnesses to an assault. The models were cutting their eyes from her to Sebastian. Lark exhaled and measured her words.

"First you authorized markdown money to be deducted without telling me, knowing full well I was counting on that check. Before you left RR, we had discussed what a nice order Pat Taylor had placed. And then you stole the designs for the new collection, knowing I wouldn't have enough time to produce another line before fashion week."

"Not my problem," he simply said.

"Why are you being so vindictive? We used to have a good working relationship. What happened?" she asked, her voice cracking.

"You thought you could just fire me and…poof—" he snapped his fingers "—I'd be gone! Well, you're wrong!

Randolph on the Runway is nothing without me. Oh, and by the way, I helped to create most of the pieces in the collection, so basically I was just taking what is rightfully mine."

"It's called *stealing,* Sebastian! Those designs were company property!"

He went over to a model and adjusted her belt. "Well, they're my property now. So deal with it."

"Hello?"

Lark turned toward the door and saw an attractive young woman who was stylishly dressed come through the door.

"Hey there, Iman. You're right on time." He glared at Lark. "Come on in." Sebastian walked right past Lark as if she weren't there and greeted the blogger with a kiss on each cheek.

"Oh my God, I love this jumpsuit!" Iman said, making a beeline straight to the model.

"Isn't it to die for?" Sebastian chimed in.

"Yes, it is. I love the asymmetrical neckline."

Lark stood there in disbelief as she watched the blogger fawn all over the design Sebastian had stolen. Lark was about to speak up and reveal the truth, but the blogger took out her cell phone and started snapping pictures of each piece.

"I'm uploading these pics to my blog right now. I have a ton of followers and the buzz will be on the street within minutes. Sebastian, you're a genius!" The blogger then turned to Lark and said, "I see you're already wearing his jumpsuit. It looks fab on you. Mind if I take your picture?"

"Please don't." Lark put her hand in front of the phone. "These aren't his designs. They belong…"

"Excuse me?" the blogger asked.

"Iman, let me show you this piece," Sebastian said, cutting Lark off and walking over to one of the models. "What do you think?"

"Love, love, love it! This pantsuit is so retro," she said, snapping a picture.

Lark turned around and walked out the door. Trying to explain to the blogger that Sebastian had stolen RR's designs was useless. She felt sick to her stomach. All of the hard work she and her team had done re-inputting the designs was for nothing. There was no way her company could go into production with the same designs Sebastian was using. RR would be the laughingstock of the industry. She had to face the cold hard facts... Randolph on the Runway was through.

Chapter 24

Lark was so despondent that she couldn't bring herself to go back to work. Sebastian had stolen the company's designs. Now Randolph on the Runway was without a collection for the spring/summer shows. With sales plummeting faster than the temperature during the polar vortex, she was counting on the new collection to reinvigorate the company. If it weren't for social media, Lark would probably have filed an injunction against Sebastian and stopped him from showing the line, but now that was moot. Pictures had been taken of his clothes and been spread all over the internet. Lark knew if she made a claim against Sebastian, it would be his word against hers. He had made a smart move by presenting his collection to the blogger and getting instant exposure. Lark had completely underestimated Sebastian. She knew he was upset about being fired, but she hadn't thought he would lash out in such a vindictive and evil way.

Lark walked slowly in a daze along West Broadway, as people whizzed past her on the sidewalk. She didn't have a destination in mind, so she moseyed aimlessly until she came upon a coffee shop. Lark went inside and found an empty table.

"Good afternoon, miss. What can I get for you?" the waitress asked.

"I'll have a cup of coffee."

"Is that all?"

"Yes."

As she sat there and gazed out of the window, she couldn't help but think of Sebastian passing off RR's spring/summer collection as his own. The more she thought about it, the madder she became. Lark needed to talk to someone. She didn't want to go crying on Dash's shoulder. He had already bailed her out once. There was only one person she felt comfortable confiding in, and that was Darcy. She took the phone out of her purse and dialed her friend.

"Hi, Darcy. Are you busy?" Lark asked in a barely audible voice.

"Just returning some emails. What's wrong? You sound upset."

"Are you at home?"

"Yes. Are you okay?"

"Not really. Can I come over? I don't want to talk about this over the phone."

"Of course. Come right over."

"I'm on my way."

Lark didn't wait for the waitress to bring the coffee. She put a few dollars on the table and left.

Traffic was bumper-to-bumper on West Broadway, so Lark walked to the West Village, where Darcy owned a three-storied Victorian brownstone. The time she spent walking helped to calm her down. She no longer felt like crying, regurgitating or committing murder. Her head was clearer. Hopefully between her and Darcy, they could come up with a viable solution to her problem. Sebastian had committed the ultimate betrayal. Stealing RR's entire collection had not only been unethical, but it had also been a criminal act, and she was going to find some way to make him pay.

Lark stood on Darcy's stoop and rang her bell. She could see Darcy coming toward her through the wood-and-beveled-glass doors.

"Come on in. I made a pitcher of Manhattans. I could tell by your tone you probably could use a drink."

Darcy had introduced Lark to the old-fashioned drink years before. She had told Lark that since she was a working woman, it was time to give up the kiddie cocktails and drink like big girl.

"I sure could." Lark followed Darcy through the double doors into the front parlor, which was furnished with antiques and oil paintings. She took a seat on a burgundy crushed-velvet sofa and watched as Darcy shook the silver shaker and poured two martini glasses full of the liquor.

"Here you go," Darcy said, handing her the glass. "To what ails you."

"I'll drink to that." Lark drank half of her cocktail in one gulp.

"So tell me. What's going on?" Darcy asked, refilling Lark's glass.

Lark exhaled hard. "Where should I start? When Dash and I were in Italy, there was a computer breach at the company and all of the designs for the new collection were wiped out. Luckily, we had hard copies and were able to reinsert the designs."

"Thank goodness for the old-school ways."

"Yes, that's exactly what I thought. But inputting the designs proved to be a monumental waste of time."

"Why? You guys didn't get them in before the production deadline?"

"We met the deadline by working nearly day and night."

"Then what's the problem?" Darcy asked, taking a sip of her cocktail.

"I read on Iman M's blog that Sebastian was previewing his line today, so I went by his loft to surprise him. But I'm the one who got the surprise of my life!"

"What happened?"

"Sebastian hacked into RR's system and stole the designs for the new collection," Lark said, shaking her head in disgust.

"Are you sure he stole your designs?"

"I'm positive. He had a mini fashion show at his loft with the pieces from RR's spring/summer collection."

"You've got to be kidding!"

"I wish I were. I should have suspected that he was the one who hacked into the system. It didn't even cross my mind that Sebastian could be that tech savvy. When he was with the company, he was always complaining about having to use the CAD system. He was old-school and hated computers. Anyway, the blogger took pictures of the line and uploaded them to the internet, so basically—"

"You have to scrap your entire spring/summer collection," Darcy said.

"Yep!"

"What a lowlife! I'm shocked Sebastian would go to such extreme measures to get back at you. He's talented in his own right. He didn't have to steal from you."

"In essence, he told me that since he cocreated the line, he was entitled to the collection. I'm still having a hard time processing all of this." Lark finished her drink and poured another. "And that's not all he's done."

"Don't tell me there's more."

"On his last day, he authorized markdown money to be deducted from a payment I was expecting without telling me."

"Oh, no, he didn't!" Darcy looked shocked. "How much was deducted?"

"Seventy grand."

"That's substantial. I hate when buyers deduct markdown money. That happened to me once before and I could barely make payroll. I'm sure you had that money earmarked."

"I certainly did. If it weren't for Dash, the company would be seriously in the red."

"Why? What did he do?"

"He wrote out a check for one hundred thousand and gave it to me as if it were no big deal."

"You're kidding. He has that type of money? I thought you said he was a young designer. I assumed he was struggling like the majority of us did during the lean years of our early career."

"Dash's family has billions. He's a trust-fund baby with tons of his own money in the bank. He's a generous soul who gives to charities. You'd think with all of that money, he'd be a pompous jerk, but he's down-to-earth and isn't arrogant in the least. He's really special."

"Wow! I had no idea he had that type of wealth. Have you told him about Sebastian stealing the collection?"

"No."

"Why not? From what you're telling me, I'm sure he'd be more than willing to help."

"What can he do? It's too late to design another collection with fashion week close at hand," Lark said, sounding totally defeated.

"I have a plan that just might work. Call Dash and have him meet us over here."

"I don't know, Darcy…"

"Do you want Sebastian to win?"

With the mere mention of that traitor's name, Lark perked up. "Hell, no!" She took out her phone and dialed Dash's number.

"Hey, babe, where are you?" Dash asked. "We're all waiting for you to start the production meeting."

"Give everyone my apologies and postpone the meeting. I'm at Darcy's place. I need you to come over here as soon as possible."

"Is everything okay?"

"Not really. I'll explain when you get here." She gave him the address and ended the call.

While they waited for Dash to arrive, Lark and Darcy went into the kitchen and Darcy whipped together chicken pesto pasta and a salad. She also put on a pot of coffee, saying they would probably be working late into the night. Lark sat at the yellow Formica kitchen table, gazing out of the window while Darcy cooked.

"I need to apologize to you," Darcy said, tossing the penne and sauce together.

"For what?"

"When we were at Balthazar, I gave you a hard time

regarding Dash. To be honest, I thought you had made a huge mistake by getting involved with one of your employees. I didn't want him to take advantage of you. But from the sound of it, Dash has been a lifesaver. I can't wait to meet him."

Lark went over to the stove, where Darcy stood, and gave her a hug. "Thanks for being so candid. Between you and Dash, I know whatever idea we come up with to salvage the collection will be a winner." Lark had a newfound sense of hope. She could see brightness through the gloomy cloud that Sebastian had cast over them.

The bell rang, interrupting their tender moment, and Darcy excused herself to go to the front. A few moments later, Lark could hear Dash and Darcy walking toward the back and chatting like old friends.

"I love the way you redid the crown molding," Dash said.

"It took me two years to strip the layers of paint off the woodwork. Renovating this place has been a labor of love," Darcy replied.

"Well, you've done a stellar job. Hey, babe," Dash said, coming over to Lark and planting a kiss on her cheek.

"Listen to you two gabbing away like you've known each other for years," Lark said with a smile on her face. She was glad her two favorite people in the world were hitting it off. She knew Darcy could be hypercritical when it came to men.

"I don't say this often, but this guy is a keeper. He's handsome and smart, and I can tell by the way he looks at you that he genuinely cares for you," Darcy said, as if Dash weren't standing there.

"Your instincts are spot-on, Darcy. Lark is extremely

important to me. I know you two are close, and your approval means a lot."

"I have one more thing to say on the subject of your relationship, and that is…don't hurt my girl," Darcy said with a stern expression on her face.

Dash hugged Lark to his side. "She's my girl, too, and I wouldn't dream of causing her any undue stress."

"You two are the best. Now, let's get to the reason why we're here." Lark filled Dash in on Sebastian's latest sabotage.

"Where is his loft?" Dash asked.

"In Tribeca. Why?"

"I want to go over there and rip him a new one. Nobody messes with my girl like that," Dash said, fuming.

"I've got a better idea. Between the three of us, we can brainstorm and design an awesome collection in no time. Then get it into production and still be able to present during fashion week," Darcy said.

"We don't have the manpower or the square footage to pull that off. We'll need at least three times the staff to manufacture an entire new collection with such a short window of time. Besides, RR's production facility isn't big enough to house that many people," Lark said.

"Since my company isn't presenting a collection for the spring/summer shows, we can use my production warehouse for the space we'll need to hire extra sewers. I'm sure with a team of seamstresses we can get the line done in time," Darcy suggested.

"That's an excellent idea. The only problem is financing. It'll take a hefty endowment to create a new collection at the last minute," Lark explained.

"Finding capital won't be a problem. Randolph on the Runway has a five-hundred-thousand-dollar line of credit with UBS, and more money is available if we need it," Dash said matter-of-factly.

Lark looked at him strangely. "We don't have any accounts with the Union Bank of Switzerland. I wish we did—that type of capital would surely come in handy right about now."

"As of yesterday, we do. I had my private banker open an account to correct any financial hiccups the company might encounter. The funds have been transferred and are ready for withdrawal."

"You can't be serious." Lark sank down on one of the kitchen chairs. Her mind was reeling. She couldn't believe what Dash had done

"Dash, this is fantastic news! You are an amazing young man. I'll coordinate the seamstresses so they're ready to start once the designs are complete. Let me go and get my sketch pads so we can get to work." Darcy rushed out of the kitchen.

"Why didn't you tell me about the line of credit you opened?" Lark asked.

"I wasn't trying to deceive you, Lark, but you really didn't want to take my check, so I had a feeling that you would object to the line of credit. I had a sneaking suspicion Sebastian might try something else and I wanted to be ready in case he did. Don't worry about the money. Like I told you before, I'd rather put my money to good use than have it sit in a bank."

"Dash, you're going to make me cry. No one has ever been this good to me. If it weren't for you, I would have had to withdraw RR from the show. What a major debacle that would have been."

"That's exactly what that bastard Sebastian wanted,

but we're not going to give him the satisfaction of seeing Randolph on the Runway fail."

"All I can say is *thank you*."

"You're more than welcome. And I'm going to give Vance a call and see what we can do about pressing charges against Sebastian for hacking into the computer system and stealing company property."

"Great idea! I would love to see him behind bars. Maybe he can design a lovely orange jumpsuit for his stay in the big house."

Lark didn't know what she had done to deserve a man as kind as Dash. She thought maybe it was her reward for dealing with so many losers over the course of her lifetime. Whatever force had brought Dash into her life, she was grateful beyond belief. Even if Dash didn't have a single dime to his name, Lark would have loved him. He had integrity, and that was something money couldn't buy.

Chapter 25

Darcy's production facilities in DUMBO—Down Under the Manhattan Bridge Overpass—was bustling with activity. There were forty seamstresses with their heads down, sewing rapidly. Lark, Dash and Darcy had worked nonstop for days coming up with an entire new spring/ summer collection. Their collaboration had resulted in a classic take on womenswear with a 1940s vibe. The line consisted of dresses, pantsuits and coordinates. Luckily, Sebastian hadn't gotten his paws on the custom fabric from Italy, and they were able to use the silk. Lark decided against putting a jumpsuit in the line since Sebastian was showcasing the one she had designed with the asymmetrical neckline. Lark thought it was ironic… Sebastian adamantly believed she couldn't design her way out of a paper bag, yet he was using one of her key pieces. He hadn't had a hand in designing that particular garment—it had been Lark's idea. And even if he had, all designs were property of Randolph on the Runway.

"Darcy, I can't thank you enough for letting us use your space," Lark said, walking into Darcy's office. "I have the production team over at RR working on the coordinates, but I really needed the extra help in order to get the collection finished in time."

"No problem. I'm just happy the production space was free. I didn't have the funds to go into production this season. Fortunately, my collection from last season sold well and I'll be able to stay afloat for a while."

"I have an idea!" Lark said, sitting down across from Darcy. "Why don't you think about coming back to RR?"

"You already have a lead designer. Besides, that would seem like a step backward. Thanks, but no, thanks."

"That's true, but I'm talking about you coming back with your own label under the RR umbrella. We've worked so well together these past couple of days and I think the synergy between the two brands would be a perfect marriage. It could help boost both of our sales. What do you think?"

"I would have my own design team and a separate label?"

"Yep. It could be called Darcy for RR or whatever name you come up with. You would have complete autonomy. The two brands would strengthen each other," Lark said enthusiastically.

"I like the idea. I'm in! First, we'll get your collection squared away, and then let's draw up a contract so I can start working on the new collection."

"Great! Sebastian's sabotage is turning out to be a good thing. If he hadn't stolen the designs, we wouldn't be sitting here talking about collaborating."

"We probably would have worked together again anyway, but Sebastian sped up the process. Where's Dash? I haven't seen him all day."

"He's meeting with his friend Vance, who also happens to be his attorney. Dash wanted to fill him in on what's been going on and how we can sue Sebastian for breach of contract."

"Why isn't your legal department working on that?" Darcy wanted to know.

"I cleaned house once I found out it was Sebastian who hacked into RR's computer system. I have a suspicion he was working with someone in-house in order to gain access. This may sound callous, but I let go of all the staff Sebastian befriended while he was an employee. Knowing Sebastian, he must have charmed someone into giving him the pass code or doing his dirty work, since he isn't tech savvy. I can't go through another betrayal like this. Sebastian really threw me for a loop. And I can't afford to be caught off guard again."

"No, that doesn't sound callous. You're a businesswoman and that's a wise decision. How are the plans going for the show?"

"Everything is on schedule. I've met with Michael Newell, the show coordinator, and he's selected the music for each scene. I've also met with the set designer and he's come up with an awesome concept. The only thing left to do is hire the models. Normally, I would have booked them by now, but with all the turmoil, I totally forgot. It shouldn't be a problem since I always use the same ones. Let me send Angelica a text so she can call the agency."

As Lark was texting her assistant, Vance came into the office. "Good afternoon, ladies."

"Hello. And you would be?" Darcy asked.

Lark looked up. "Hi, Vance. Darcy, this is Vance Shelton, Dash's attorney. I faxed him a copy of Sebastian's contract to look over, so we can take the next step in suing that SOB. Come in, Vance, and have a seat."

Lark had taken a liking to Vance. Although she still thought he was a ladies' man, he had proved to be a great attorney. Vance had jumped in with both feet the moment Dash had called and said that RR needed new legal representation.

"You ladies sure are looking well," Vance said, smiling at Darcy.

"Are you flirting with me, young man?" Darcy asked.

"I certainly am. You're a beautiful woman," he said boldly as he sat across from her.

"How old are you—twenty-four? Twenty-five?"

"I'm twenty-five. I'll be twenty-six in a few months."

"I'll have you know I have shoes older than you," she said, laughing.

"Don't be so quick to knock something you've never had."

Watching their exchange, Lark could see the serious expression on Vance's face. Darcy's cheeks had begun to flush red. Lark cleared her throat, interrupting their banter. "Where's Dash? I thought he was with you."

"He came by the office, but he said he had to run an errand. He told me to tell you he'll see you later."

"Oh, okay. So did you get a chance to look over Sebastian's contract?"

"I certainly did, and it's ironclad. All the designs he created while employed with RR were proprietary and belong to the company."

"Thanks. I just wanted you to confirm what I already

knew. Did you draw up the breach-of-contract lawsuit papers?" Lark asked.

Vance reached into his briefcase and handed her a large envelope. "All the paperwork is here. You just need to sign it before I can file the suit."

"Can we stop him from showing his collection in the show?" Darcy asked.

"Unfortunately not. We do not have proof it was Sebastian who hacked into the system and stole the designs. Until we have evidence to support your accusation, it's Sebastian's word against yours."

"The designs are proof enough. Pictures of his work… I mean my work, are all over the internet. I can give you my sketch pad with the original designs. That should count for something," Lark said.

"Yes, it might, but that process will be long-drawn-out. The fashion shows will be over before we'll be able to get an injunction to stop him," Vance told her.

"Damn!" Lark exclaimed.

"Don't worry. Sebastian won't get away with this. I promise you that," Vance stated. "You focus on the creative end and let me deal with the legal stuff. I might be young—" he cut his eyes at Darcy "—but I know my way around the courtroom, among other places."

"Thanks so much, Vance. I really appreciate all of your help," Lark said.

"Anytime. I've gotta run. I have to be in court in an hour, but I'll be in touch." He reached out and shook Darcy's hand. "So very nice to meet you. I hope to see you again soon."

"Be careful what you hope for," Darcy responded.

Once Vance was gone, Darcy stood, crossed the room

and closed the door. She fanned her hand across her face. "What a hottie!"

"He is handsome. Maybe you should go out on a date with him."

"Are you kidding? He's way too young for me."

"You don't have to get seriously involved with him. Don't get me wrong—I think Vance is a nice guy, but I don't think he's ready to settle down. Just get your groove on and move on. Men do it all the time. Why is it okay for a sixty-year-old man to not only date a twenty-two-year-old, but to marry her and…have kids? Take a look at some celebrities in Hollywood. I can name at least ten couples with a monumental age difference between them. Besides, who cares what other people think?"

"I guess you have a point. Maybe I will see what he's working with. It's been a while since I had an intimate encounter. I don't want to marry him, but I wouldn't mind having the cobwebs cleared out, if you know what I mean," Darcy said with a wicked smile.

"I most certainly do! Here's his office number." Lark wrote down a number on a piece of paper and handed it to Darcy.

"Now, you know I don't make the initial call to men."

"Well, there's a first time for everything. Call him and have some fun. You'll need to de-stress once the show is over," Lark said, trying to convince her friend.

"I most certainly will." Darcy took the piece of paper and put it in her purse.

For the remainder of the day Lark and Darcy pinned the sample pieces on fit models to adjust the cut of the garments, approved the finished pieces and figured out the order of the clothing for the show. They were so busy the day flew by at a rapid pace. With the clock approaching midnight, they decided to call it a night.

Lark had been so caught up with work she hadn't noticed that Dash had never made it back to the warehouse. It wasn't like him not to check in all day. She called him, but his voice mail picked up.

"Hey, babe, what happened to you today? I thought you were coming back to the warehouse. You're probably working at the office. In any event, I'm heading home. I'll talk to you later."

Lark disconnected the call, gathered her belongings and headed out. She was physically and mentally exhausted. All she wanted to do was take a shower, put on her pj's and climb into bed, and that was exactly what she planned on doing once she arrived home.

Chapter 26

Dash had spent the entire day working on a special project. After meeting with Vance, Dash was supposed to meet Lark at Darcy's production facilities, but he hurried back to the office instead. He had an appointment with the patternmaker regarding a design for the show. The piece he was working on wouldn't be produced at Darcy's. This was his baby and he wanted to personally handle every single detail. The task had taken up all of his time and he hadn't seen Lark all day. He missed her. She had gotten deep into his system and he found himself constantly craving her. Dash wanted to be near Lark all the time, and when they were apart, his soul ached. He knew beyond a shadow of a doubt he had fallen in love with Lark Randolph. Their romance had taken the express lane all the way to Blissville. Some men might have gotten scared and shied away from their true feelings, but not Dash. He knew women like Lark came around only once in a lifetime, and he wasn't going to make the mistake of letting her get away.

Dash had taken a break in his day that afternoon to purchase a few bottles of wine, a wedge of Pecorino Romano cheese, a pound of prosciutto, a ripe cantaloupe and black-olive focaccia. He didn't bother buying olive tapenade, since nobody made it better than Sophia—who used fresh olives from the family grove—so he settled on the freshly baked olive bread instead. Dash wanted to re-create the romantic picnic he and Lark had shared in Livorno. The only thing missing would be the breathtaking view of the turquoise waters. He even bought a wicker basket to hold the goodies.

After he had finished with his task, he attempted to call Lark, but his phone was dead. He had been so busy he'd forgotten to charge it. Since it was late, Dash decided against going to the warehouse. He thought Lark would surely be home by now.

He left the office, hailed a taxi downstairs and headed straight to Lark's place.

"I'm sorry, Mr. Migilio, but Ms. Randolph isn't picking up," the doorman told Dash after he arrived at her building.

"That's okay. I'll wait."

"Sure—no problem. There are seats near the elevators."

With the picnic basket in hand, he headed to the waiting area. He sat on one of the Art Deco inspired gray velvet sofas. Ten minutes passed with no sign of Lark. He was beginning to worry. Dash took out his phone to call her, but he remembered it wasn't charged. He glanced at his vintage Rolex. It was twelve-thirty. *Where is she?* he wondered.

"Dash, what are you doing here?" Lark asked, approaching him.

He stood. "Hey, babe, I was beginning to worry about you. Are you okay?" he asked, looking at her weary face.

"Just tired, that's all."

Dash watched Lark's eyes wander down to his hand. "What's in the basket?" she asked.

"It's a surprise. You'll see when we get upstairs."

He took her by the hand and they moseyed over to the elevators. "How did it go today?" he asked once they'd stepped into the elevator car.

"Very productive. Vance came by with the papers for me to sign for the lawsuit. He said we may not be able to stop Sebastian from presenting during fashion week. However, Vance assured me that Sebastian won't get away with what he's done."

"You can count on that. How was the rest of your day?"

"Good. Darcy and I made adjustments to some of the garments. The fabric we had made in Italy is so fluid that it moved over the bodies of the fit models like water. I can just see the girls strutting down the runway and the fabric floating on the breeze behind them."

"I'm not just saying this because it's my family's company, but the mill produces high-quality textiles. Our designs coupled with the exquisite material will definitely set us apart from the rest of the design houses."

"That's true. I'm really getting excited about fashion week. A few days ago, I thought there was no way RR would be able to present during the shows, but thanks to you and Darcy, the new collection is far better than the designs Sebastian stole." Lark kissed Dash on the cheek.

"Save those kisses for later." He winked.

The elevator arrived at her floor. They stepped off and walked down the hallway arm in arm.

The apartment was dark, so Lark flicked on the light switch near the front door. "Come on in and have a seat. I need to take a quick shower. I'll be right back," she said, heading off toward the master suite.

While Lark was in the bathroom, Dash went into the linen closet, found a cashmere blanket and took it off the shelf. He returned to the living room and spread the soft blanket atop the chocolate-brown suede rug.

He then went into the kitchen and sliced the cantaloupe. He found dishes, silverware and glasses for their living room picnic. With his arms full, Dash rushed back to the living room, spread out the dishes and took the contents out of the basket. He opened a bottle of red wine and poured two glasses. He leaned his back against one of the white leather sofas, sipped his wine and waited for Lark. Although Dash had had a full day, he felt reenergized now that he and Lark were together. And the last thing on his mind at the moment was sleep.

"What have we here?"

Dash looked up and nearly gasped. Lark was wearing a red lace teddy with a neckline that plunged down to her belly button. Her nipples were poking through the sheer fabric and he could see the outline of her neatly shaven triangle. "You look good enough to eat. Come, sit down." He reached for her hand.

"Aw, this is exactly like what we ate on our romantic picnic on the hill," she commented, noticing the food.

"Yep, all except for the olive tapenade. Since we can't

go back to Italy at the moment, I thought I'd bring Italy
to us. We've both been working around the clock these
past few days and I wanted to carve out a little time just
for us." Dash cut a thin slice of Pecorino Romano and
fed it to Lark. He let his fingers linger in her mouth as
she took the cheese.

"Hmm, that's good."

"Here, try the focaccia." He broke off a piece of bread
and fed it to her.

"Wow, that's so fresh. I love black olives. This picnic
was such a good idea. I feel totally relaxed. What other
goodies do you have?"

"I'm glad you're enjoying it." Dash picked up a piece
of prosciutto. He glanced down at the plate, looking for
the cantaloupe. "Oh, I left the melon in the kitchen on
the counter," Dash said.

"Don't bother. I've got two melons right here."

He watched as Lark took hold of her breasts and jig-
gled them. Dash reached out, replaced her hands with
his and moved the material from around her breasts. He
took his hands away and admired her breasts.

"You've got the best-looking nipples. They're not too
big or too small. They're the perfect mouthful." Dash
moved closer, leaned down and licked her nipples. The
right one and then the left one. He trailed his tongue
between her breasts and kissed her tender skin.

"That feels good," Lark said, lying down on the blanket.

Dash kissed Lark on the lips, then lay next to her and
wrapped her in his arms.

"I'm in love with you, Lark Randolph."

"Like Patrick Swayze said in *Ghost,* 'Ditto.'"

"'Ditto'?"

"Just kidding. I love you, too, Dash Migilio." Lark wrapped her arms around him and kissed him passionately.

That night, after making love more than once, they didn't bother moving to the bedroom; both were too exhausted to budge. They rested like two lovebirds nestled together in their own world.

Their bliss barely lasted eight hours. The next morning, instead of basking in the afterglow, Lark was on the phone with her assistant. Angelica had called Lark at home with some disturbing news.

"What do you mean all the models have been booked? Didn't you tell the agency we use those girls at every show?"

"Of course I did, but the agency said there's nothing they can do at such a short notice," Angelica responded.

"Let me call them and see what I can do," Lark said, and she hung up.

"What's going on? I could hear you yelling all the way in the bathroom," Dash said. He came into the kitchen, where Lark sat at the counter in her bathrobe.

"The models I normally use for the show have been booked. I'm calling the agency now to see what's going on." Lark punched buttons on her phone.

"Good morning, The Bella Agency."

"This is Lark Randolph. Is Bella in?"

"Hold on, please."

A few seconds later, the owner of the agency, whom Lark had known for years, was on the line. "Ciao, Lark. How are you?"

"Not good, Bella. I'm trying to book my models for the show and I've been told they're not available. I know it's last-minute, but you always put the same girls on hold for me. What happened?"

"Sebastian called and said RR wasn't presenting a collection during fashion week, so I released the girls."

"HE DID WHAT?"

"Didn't he tell you?" Bella asked.

"Sebastian is no longer employed with RR, and he has no say in what goes on with my company!"

"Oh. I didn't know."

Lark held the phone for a second. "Yes, I'm sure he didn't bother to volunteer that information."

"I wish I could help, Lark, but the only girls I have available are print models with no runway experience."

"No worries, Bella. Listen, I've gotta run. 'Bye."

"What's happened now?" Dash asked.

"That SOB Sebastian called the agency and had them release the models for my show."

"You've got to be kidding!"

"I wish I were. The show is in two days. What am I going to do now?" Lark paused for a few moments. "Wait a minute…all is not lost. I have a good friend in Milan who has a modeling agency. He only has the crème de la crème. His models are all seasoned and can work a runway like Naomi Campbell. I'll call him and have a stable of girls flown over."

"Brilliant idea. Don't worry about the cost. Even if you have to pay an extra fee for the last-minute booking, it'll be worth having experienced models on the runway."

"Thanks, baby. You are the absolute best!"

"Anything for you, Lark."

"Let me shower. I want to get to the warehouse as soon as possible. The clock is ticking and we have a gazillion more things to do before the big day," she said, hopping off the stool and heading toward the master suite.

As Dash made himself a cup of coffee, he thought about Sebastian. *The dude is relentless. He has to be stopped once and for all.*

Chapter 27

The engraved invitations to Randolph on the Runway's spring/summer show had been personally delivered by messenger—a touch she thought would set RR's show apart from the masses—to the fashion editors at the leading newspapers and magazines, buyers at the major retailers, a handful of fashion-forward celebrities who were fixtures at the shows, and Park Avenue socialites. Lark had spared no expense with the preparations. She had hired a world-renowned set designer who had created a Cirque du Soleil–type stage with colorful drapery and whimsical props. The music was to be a mixture of Caribbean and African beats laced with bebop. Lark wanted their show to have a lasting effect—to create a buzz long after the lights dimmed and the guests departed.

The big day had finally arrived and Lark was filled

with the excitement of an expectant mother. She, Darcy, Dash and their staff had labored intensely over the collection, working double-time in order to pull off the impossible. This collection of clothing had a special meaning for Lark. As the years passed, she could always remember this new line as the catalyst that brought her and Dash together. Although she had faced many challenges—from finding a silk manufacturer at the last minute, to re-creating an entire new line with little time to spare—she couldn't change a thing. This was her baby, and the time had arrived for the big reveal.

Fashion week was in full swing with massive white tents erected at Lincoln Center. The entire outdoor area had been completely transformed into a fashion oasis. Stylish guests were swarming about like busy bees before making their way inside the designated tents. Some members of the press remained camped outside, while others went inside to report on the various shows. Randolph on the Runway's tent was sandwiched between designers Nanette Lepore and Vivienne Tam, two heavy hitters in the industry. RR was in good company, and Lark felt great about their positioning.

Backstage at Randolph on the Runway was organized chaos. There was a frenzy of activity with models, wardrobe stylists, hairstylists, makeup artists, designers, assistants and photographers frantically toiling away before the proverbial curtain went up and the show began. Some of the models Lark had flown in from Milan were sitting in director's chairs getting their faces painted and their hair teased. The others were being fussed over by stylists who were fitting them for the first scene. Lark's friend in Milan had come through for her. Not only had he sent his best models, but he also hadn't charged her an outrageous fee. Lark was beyond pleased with the models, who were of various races.

"The waist on that dress should be cinched in more," Lark told Loghan, the stylist.

"Like this?" Loghan asked, pulling fabric from the back.

"Yes, that's much better. You can see the silhouette of the garment better."

Loghan took a couple of pins from a tiny cushion on her wrist and quickly made the adjustment.

Lark inspected the other models, giving her approval, before moving on to the racks of clothing to take one last look at the collection. She removed one of the dresses and held it high in the air, visually inspecting the piece.

"Looks good and so do you," Dash said, coming up behind her.

Lark wore a black pantsuit, sans blouse, from the collection. The two-button jacket was cropped at the waist, and the pant leg flared dramatically. She wore a triple strand of pearls around her neck. Her hair was gelled back behind her ears and she wore a pair of black cat-eye glasses. Her look was edgy yet sexy.

Lark turned the garment around to the back. "You think so?"

"Absolutely. The way the fabric is ruched along the right side will expose the leg all the way up to the thigh, giving a dramatic presentation as the model struts down the catwalk."

Lark exhaled, releasing a breath of tension. "You're right. I don't know why I'm second-guessing myself. Even if I didn't like the gathering effect of the material, there's little I can do about it now."

"If you really hated it, we could cut it off and make the maxi dress into a mini."

"That's why I love you. You're full of fabulous ideas."

"That's the only reason?" Dash asked with a naughty glint in his eyes.

Lark couldn't help but chuckle. "Yes…that, too." She took in Dash's appearance. He wore a white shirt and a tailored black suit that fit his body to perfection. The legs of the pants were slim and the jacket hugged his shoulders. Lark's mind flashed back to the first time she had laid eyes on Dash and the attraction she felt toward him. She had initially been drawn to his good looks, but it was Dash's sense of integrity that drew him to her.

"The models look terrific. I love the idea of airbrushing their faces white and having their lipstick be different colors," Dash commented.

"Thanks. Those girls can pull it off—they're runway superstars. The chocolate-skinned girl sitting in the chair getting her face painted just won Model of the Year at the Paris Fashion Awards. She's from the Congo and speaks four languages."

"So much for that old falsehood of models being dumb as a box of rocks."

"Maybe some of them are, but my friend in Milan told me this girl studied at the Sorbonne and didn't start her modeling career until after she graduated."

"Good for her."

As they were talking, Dash's cell phone rang. "Hello?… Okay, we'll be right out." He ended the call. "Come on. There's something you have to see," Dash said, taking Lark by the arm.

"Wait a minute! I can't leave. The show is getting ready to start," she said, pulling away.

"We have time. Trust me, this is important."

"Hold on a second. Let me see if any of the bigwigs have been seated yet," Lark said, going to peek out of the curtain. She poked her head out and took a quick look. "Oh my gosh! You won't believe who is out there!" she exclaimed.

"Who?"

"The publisher of *Threads,* the new fashion magazine, and sitting right next to her is André the fashion editor, looking fabulous as ever! Do you know what it means to have them sitting front row at our show? They could have gone to any number of shows but they're here! If they like the collection, we'll most likely be mentioned in *Threads,* which could increase our bottom line significantly," Lark said, sounding giddy and excited.

"That's great, babe. Now come on." Dash took her by the hand and led her out the back way.

Outside, the crowds from earlier had dissipated. Only a few reporters and photographers remained.

"What are we doing out here?" Lark asked, sounding annoyed.

"You'll see in a minute."

Lark tapped her foot in frustration. "Dash, I really need to get back inside."

"I know. Don't worry. We won't miss the start of the show. You'll want to see this, trust me."

No sooner had Dash said the words than Lark noticed a man being brought out of one of the tents in handcuffs. He was escorted by two uniformed police officers on each side. She stepped forward, taking a closer look. "Is that Sebastian?"

"Yep, it sure is."

The few photographers remaining instantly started

snapping pictures of the designer wearing the silver city-issued bracelets.

"Wait a minute…how did this happen? Vance told me the shows would be over by the time Sebastian got his just due," Lark said, watching as one of the police officers opened the back door of the squad car and helped Sebastian inside.

"Yes, that would have been true if I hadn't followed a hunch I had."

"What kind of hunch?"

"Remember the meeting we had with the division heads when we returned from Italy?"

"Yes. What about it?"

"Edward, the head of IT, was being extremely vague and acting clueless as to how and why our system had been hacked into. I know for a fact computer geeks are on top of the latest viruses. They know before the rest of the population what threats are lurking around waiting to strike. So, when he said a Trojan virus had wiped out our CAD program, I became suspicious and hired a forensic expert who specializes in computer hacking."

"Why didn't you tell me this before now?"

"You had so much on your plate, dealing with re-creating a new collection. I didn't want to get your hopes up in case my hunch was wrong."

"Did he find out anything?"

"He sure did. He tracked Edward's IP address from his computer and found that it was Edward who'd erased all of the design files, but not before he uploaded them to a jump drive and gave it to Sebastian."

"Oh my God! Why on earth would he do that?" Lark asked in sheer amazement.

"From the emails between Edward and Sebastian,

which my investigator uncovered, it appears the two of them are lovers and have been for years…"

"Wait a minute! Edward is married and has three kids!"

"Apparently Edward has been duping his wife as well as the company."

"Wow!" Lark said, shaking her head. "I wish I would have known before now. I would have fired Edward right along with Sebastian."

"Don't worry. The police are at Edward's home as we speak, escorting him to the station. They are both being arrested for computer espionage, which is a serious offense, with hefty jail time."

"Good! That's exactly what they deserve. Dash, I can't thank you enough for what you've done for RR and for me," Lark said, tears welling up in her eyes.

"It was nothing. I'm just glad I was there to help. Otherwise, Sebastian would have probably gotten away with sabotaging the company, which would have been a shame."

The police car drove off and they watched it disappear in the distance.

"Come on. Let's get back in there before the show starts," Dash said, looping his arm with Lark's.

As they made their way back inside the tent, Lark once again thanked her lucky stars for Dash. He had solved the mystery of how Sebastian had stolen the company's designs and she was elated. Her nemesis had been caught and he could no longer taunt her. Sebastian's numerous attempts at trying to derail RR's new line had proved futile and he had finally gotten what he deserved. This day was getting better and better. Now the time had finally come to unveil RR's new collection, a collection that Lark was sure would be a smash hit.

Chapter 28

"Where have you guys been? The show is getting ready to start!" Darcy exclaimed as she rushed up to them.

"We were outside watching Sebastian be escorted out by the police," Lark said, clapping her hands.

"What? Are you serious?"

"As a heart attack." Lark reiterated what Dash had told her about Sebastian and Edward.

"Get the hell out of here! I remember when Edward was hired years ago. He was a newlywed with a baby on the way." Darcy shook her head. "Sometimes you really don't know what a person is capable of, do you? Good work, Dash."

"It was my pleasure. Getting taken away by the police during fashion week is exactly what he deserved. Even if he never sees the inside of a prison, his career is over. I saw reporters snapping pictures and I'm sure he'll be featured in the style section tomorrow," Dash said.

"He'll be featured, all right…as an orange-jumpsuit-wearing thief!" Lark commented.

"I can just see the headlines now… Designer Arrested at Fashion Week. I'm sure Sebastian was expecting press but not that kind," Darcy said.

As they were talking, the lights dimmed, the music started and a group of models positioned themselves near the curtain.

"It's showtime! Let's take our places out front," Lark said.

"You two go ahead. I'll be right out," Dash replied.

"Where are you going? Don't you want to see the show?" Lark asked.

Dash saw the shocked expression on Lark's face. "I need to take care of one last detail. Go ahead. I won't be long."

"Uh…okay."

Lark and Darcy slipped through the side of the curtain and went out front. Once they were gone, Dash headed toward the back to check on the finale piece.

The beat of the drums was loud and intense and Lark could feel her body vibrating from the music. She and Darcy stood near the stage and watched in anticipation as the models strutted out one by one wearing the fabulous garments she and her team had created. The custom floral silk fabric of the dresses floated on the breeze as the models glided down the catwalk and twirled on their heels. Overhead spotlights captured their painted faces, making the entire presentation even more dramatic. From where Lark stood, she could see the guests' reactions. Some were smiling, obviously enjoying the show, and some people were stoic, showing no emotion. "Do you think the publisher from *Threads* likes the collection so far?" Lark whispered in Darcy's ear.

Darcy glanced in the woman's direction. "I don't know. She's a hard read. But the fact she's at your show is a good sign. From what I've heard, Ms. Lancaster is extremely selective about which shows she attends. The fact that she's here at all is a good sign."

"You're right. That's exactly what I thought earlier." Lark focused her attention back on the show.

The music morphed from an African/Caribbean beat into a 1940s up-tempo bebop rhythm, with the sounds of Dizzy Gillespie blowing his trumpet. A second set of models marched out wearing menswear-inspired 1940s pantsuits. The suits were made out of the custom silk, which made them look extremely feminine. The floral pattern was quite small, giving off a solid look from a distance.

"I'm on pins and needles wondering what the buyers are thinking. My heart is beating so fast," Lark admitted.

"Mine is, too. I'm not just saying this because I'm your friend, but this show is amazing. Your idea to mesh the '40s vibe with custom prints with an African-beat twist was genius. I'm certain the sales from this collection will be off the charts," Darcy said.

"Thanks. I hope you're right. This is one collection I'll never forget. All the pains we went through to create the new line were well worth it. The last scene is coming up. I can't wait to celebrate. After all the upheaval, I could surely use a drink. I had Angelica arrange a small after-party on the rooftop at the hotel across the street."

"Sounds great. Will Vance be there?"

"He most certainly will. I had a feeling that you were not going to call him, so I invited him to the party. You never know—you guys just might make a love connection."

"Stranger things have happened." Darcy chuckled.

Lark and Darcy watched as the models came out wearing swimsuits, some with silk sarongs covering their bottoms and some without. The two-piece floral bikinis looked like mere strips of material on the models' slim bodies.

"I wish I could wear one of those," Darcy whispered.

"You can. You still have a great figure."

"I wouldn't dare wear a bikini in public."

"You could always sport one for Vance. I'm sure he'd love to see you in next to nothing," Lark teased.

"I'm glad you invited him to the party. I'm going to take your advice and give him a chance. I'm not looking to fall in love, but I wouldn't mind having a handsome boy toy at my disposal—if he's interested in that."

"My, my, my… Well, haven't you evolved? There was a time when you wouldn't have dreamed of dating a younger man."

"Don't remind me. I wasted so many years abiding by my self-made rules, I missed out on love. I might not ever get married, but one thing is for sure… I plan to have some hot, kinky sex in the very near future."

"Good for you, Darcy. Men do it all the time. I don't

see any reason why we as women can't enjoy the same pleasures!"

"We can, and I will."

The show was almost over. Lark looked toward the stage, and the bathing suit–clad models were gone. The finale piece was up next, which was an evening dress she had personally designed. She was excited to see the crowd's reaction. Her eyes shifted from the stage to the front row as she waited for the model to appear.

"Nice design," Darcy whispered once the model appeared.

The gown was made of the numerous fabric swatches representing the entire collection. The result was a patchwork of different patterns and colors. The sleek floor-length dress hugged the model's body like a second skin.

"You really like it?"

"Yes, I love it. Kudos… Great job!"

Lark could not have been more pleased the show had gone off without a hitch. As she and Darcy waited for all the models to return to the stage for final showing, Lark heard the music change into a song that wasn't on the playlist. She had gone over every piece of music with the coordinator and knew the order of each song. Lark didn't know why the finale song was different and thought that maybe the DJ had mixed up the order.

"I didn't know there were two gowns in the show," Darcy commented.

Lark whipped her head around and looked at the stage. Her mouth dropped. This wasn't one of her designs. She watched in a state of shock as the model from the Congo— sans face paint—waltzed down the catwalk in a snow-white wedding gown with a six-foot-long train trailing behind her. The model held a bouquet of jade-green roses tied with a long, flowing ribbon made from the same silk as the collection.

"What a beautiful dress," Darcy whispered.

"Yes, it is, but it's not from the line," Lark answered.

Lark watched as the model strutted to the end of the runway, tossed the bouquet into the crowd and struck a haughty pose, with her hand on her slim hip. The second the model froze, Dash appeared from behind the curtain.

"Thank you all for coming to RR's spring/summer show. I'm Dash Migilio, the lead designer. I'd like to introduce you to the creative genius behind the collection… Lark, will you please come onstage?"

Lark was frozen. She hadn't expected this.

"Go ahead. What are you waiting for?" Darcy said, giving her friend a gentle nudge.

Lark began moving, but it felt as if she were walking in a fog. She climbed the four steps at the side of the stage and walked slowly until she was standing next to Dash.

"I know this is a bit out of the ordinary for a fashion show, but…" He reached into the breast pocket of his blazer and produced a tiny, robin's egg–blue box. Dash dropped down to one knee. "Lark Randolph, will you marry me?" he asked, opening the lid of the box.

Lark stared down at the huge rock of a ring. The overhead lights made the diamond sparkle like a trillion stars in the night sky. "Yes…yes, I'll marry you!"

Dash stood, wrapped Lark in his arms and then tenderly kissed her lips. The crowd erupted into applause. Flashes from cameras flickered as they sealed their engagement.

The finale to Randolph on the Runway's spring/
summer show would no doubt be the talked-about event
for months to come, garnering press from the United
States to Europe. Lark and Dash were officially the
darlings of Seventh Avenue.

* * * * *

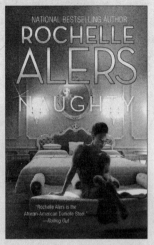

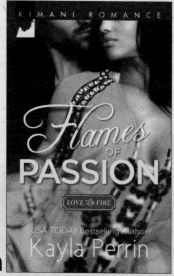

REQUEST YOUR FREE BOOKS!

2 FREE NOVELS PLUS 2 FREE GIFTS!

KIMANI™
ROMANCE

Love's ultimate destination!

Will her vacation
fling turn into a
forever love?

All of Me

SHERYL LISTER

Declaring a "dating hiatus" was an easy decision for teacher
Karen Morris. She intends to unwind and enjoy a luxurious
Caribbean cruise solo, but businessman Damian Bradshaw
manages to change her mind. They ignite an insatiable need
that neither can deny… Will the promise of a bright future
be enough to rehabilitate their reluctant hearts?

Available January 2015 wherever books are sold!